ALLEN COUNTY PUBLIC LIBRARY

3 1833 05292 3254

S0-BKR-961

ome people are ... and I'm not."

Max sounded so certain, Casey couldn't help but ask. "What's wrong with marriage?"

"Nothing. It's just not for me. I want a woman who feels the same way—one who values her independence as much as I value mine."

Independence. A heady word. Something Casey hadn't experienced much until she'd left Chicago.

And now she was here in Crested Butte. Walking with a man who believed a woman who made her own decisions and lived her own life was a wonderful thing. Had she ever dreamed of finding something so perfect?

"Why are you looking at me that way?" he asked.

She blinked. "Why am I looking at you what way?"

"As if you're not sure whether to measure me for a straitjacket or kiss me."

She smiled and leaned toward him. "Why don't we start with the kiss?"

NOV 0 7 2007

Dear Reader,

Crested Butte, Colorado, is one of my favorite places on earth, so I was thrilled to have the chance to feature the town in my first book for Harlequin American Romance. Most of the places and all the festivals mentioned in the book are real, but the characters are purely creations of my imagination. The only thing they share with the real-life residents of Crested Butte is a strong sense of community, friendship and fun.

I love books about people starting over in a new place, with a new job and a new outlook on life. My heroine, Casey, embraces the chance to live life on her own terms, but she doesn't realize how much her fresh start will inspire those around her.

I had so much fun writing this book. I hope you'll have as much fun reading it. I love to hear from readers. You can e-mail me at Cindi@CindiMyers.com or write to me at P.O. Box 991, Bailey, CO 80421. Be sure to stop by my Web site at www.CindiMyers.com to find out about my upcoming books, including the follow-up to *Marriage on Her Mind, The Right Mr. Wrong,* to be released February 2008.

Happy reading!

Cindi Myers

NOV 0 7 2007

Marriage on Her Mind

CINDI MYERS

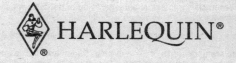

HARLEQUIN®

TORONTO • NEW YORK • LONDON
AMSTERDAM • PARIS • SYDNEY • HAMBURG
STOCKHOLM • ATHENS • TOKYO • MILAN • MADRID
PRAGUE • WARSAW • BUDAPEST • AUCKLAND

If you purchased this book without a cover you should be aware that this book is stolen property. It was reported as "unsold and destroyed" to the publisher, and neither the author nor the publisher has received any payment for this "stripped book."

ISBN-13: 978-0-373-75186-0
ISBN-10:   0-373-75186-9

MARRIAGE ON HER MIND

Copyright © 2007 by Cynthia Myers.

All rights reserved. Except for use in any review, the reproduction or utilization of this work in whole or in part in any form by any electronic, mechanical or other means, now known or hereafter invented, including xerography, photocopying and recording, or in any information storage or retrieval system, is forbidden without the written permission of the publisher, Harlequin Enterprises Limited, 225 Duncan Mill Road, Don Mills, Ontario M3B 3K9, Canada.

This is a work of fiction. Names, characters, places and incidents are either the product of the author's imagination or are used fictitiously, and any resemblance to actual persons, living or dead, business establishments, events or locales is entirely coincidental.

This edition published by arrangement with Harlequin Books S.A.

® and TM are trademarks of the publisher. Trademarks indicated with ® are registered in the United States Patent and Trademark Office, the Canadian Trade Marks Office and in other countries.

www.eHarlequin.com

Printed in U.S.A.

ABOUT THE AUTHOR

When Cindi Myers is not writing, she loves spending time out of doors. An avid downhill skier, she enjoys hiking and camping in the summer. She lives in the mountains southwest of Denver with her husband and two dogs, all of whom accompany her on most of her outdoor adventures.

Books by Cindi Myers

HARLEQUIN NEXT
MY BACKWARDS LIFE
THE BIRDMAN'S DAUGHTER

HARLEQUIN SIGNATURE SELECT
LEARNING CURVES
BOOTCAMP
  "Flirting with an Old Flame"

HARLEQUIN ANTHOLOGY
A WEDDING IN PARIS
  "Picture Perfect"

Don't miss any of our special offers. Write to us at the following address for information on our newest releases.

Harlequin Reader Service
U.S.: 3010 Walden Ave., P.O. Box 1325, Buffalo, NY 14269
Canadian: P.O. Box 609, Fort Erie, Ont. L2A 5X3

To the people of Crested Butte, Colorado

Chapter One

More than once in the past few weeks, Casey Jernigan had wondered if she was losing her mind. What was a Chicago-born-and-bred woman like her doing packing everything she owned in the back of her RAV4 and heading halfway across the country to take a job in a small town she knew nothing about?

Sitting in her car at the city limits of Crested Butte, Colorado, on a clear April morning, Casey wavered between hysterical laughter and abject panic. Though spring was fast approaching in the Midwest, here snow still lay in drifts to the rooflines, and passing cars were adorned with ski racks and snowboards. As she watched, a snowplow rumbled by, colored lights flashing as it scraped the roadway bare.

But the thing that most made Casey doubt her sanity was the dragon.

It rose, thirty feet long and fifteen feet tall, silver and gleaming in the bright afternoon sun. Neck outstretched, wings unfurled, it lunged toward the man who cowered before it. Saint George—surely it was Saint George—cringed before the dragon's onslaught, his shining armor, upraised sword and shield seeming a poor defense against the giant beast.

As defenseless as Casey suddenly felt in this remote place where she knew no one and no one knew her. At the time she'd accepted the position as the assistant director of marketing for the Crested Butte chamber of commerce, the chance to make a completely fresh start had been the primary attraction of the job. Not to mention there was something so romantic and exciting about living in a ski town in the mountains. She'd pictured handsome ski instructors and laughing children, building snowmen and cuddling before crackling fires with cups of hot chocolate.

Dragons—and this sick feeling of being far out of her element—had never figured into her dreams.

Sighing, she put the Toyota in gear and rolled slowly toward downtown Crested Butte. Elevation 8,885 feet, proclaimed the city-limits sign. Never mind the population. What was important here was the elevation. In the distance, Casey could see the mountains of Crested Butte Ski Resort, like meringue peaks on a giant pie.

She checked the directions on the computer printout on the seat beside her and searched the street signs for Elk Avenue. She'd been assured that the apartment she'd rented sight unseen was easy to find. "Right on the main drag," her new boss at the chamber, Heather Allison, had said. "You'll be able to walk to work."

Elk Avenue proved to be a collection of colorful Victorian storefronts arrayed behind towering snowdrifts. The sidewalk snaked between the drifts like a carnival maze. Casey checked her directions again and guided the Toyota to a stop in front of a bright pink-and-turquoise building with the number 27 out front. Mad Max's Snowboards and Bicycle Rental, proclaimed the sign over the door.

Mad Max? Snowboards? Where was the apartment building within walking distance of the office? The dizzy feeling of being out of place returned. Obviously, she'd written the address down wrong. But she might as well get out of the car and ask. Besides, after hours of driving she could stand to stretch her legs.

A string of sleigh bells on the back of the door to the shop jangled as Casey stepped over the threshold. A fat golden retriever stood and ambled over to her, tail wagging slowly. "Hello," Casey said, scratching the dog behind the ear. "Is anybody else here?"

"That's Molly. She's the official greeter." A smiling man with shaggy brown hair and broad shoulders emerged from a back room. He was dressed in faded jeans and a red-and-black plaid flannel shirt over a green sweater. His face was sunburned and alive with a smile that fairly bowled her over with its welcome. She stared at him for a moment—into eyes the brilliant blue of the Colorado sky. In the small part of her brain that wasn't preoccupied with admiring him, a warning sounded *Danger! Danger! Danger!* The *last* thing she needed right now was to lose her head over some handsome guy. Even if he did look as though he could have posed for one of those charity calendars—Modern Day Mountain Man or something like that.

"Let me guess. You're Casey Jernigan," he said.

"How did you know my name?" she asked, trying not to show how nervous the idea made her.

"Saw the Illinois plates on your car," he said. "And the ficus tree on the front seat gave you away. Not many people vacation with their houseplants."

She laughed. It was either that or admit she was freaked out that he'd spotted her for a newcomer so easily. But then again, Crested Butte *was* a small town, with a year-round population of fifteen hundred that easily swelled to six thousand during ski season—or so the visitor's guide she'd received from the chamber of commerce told her.

"I *am* Casey Jernigan," she said, offering her hand.

"Max Overbridge." He shook her hand with a firm, hearty grip.

"Nice to meet you, Max. And Molly." She smiled at the dog. "I've rented an apartment somewhere around here and can't find it. Maybe you can point me in the right direction."

"That would be right over our heads," Max said. "Park around back and I'll help you with your things."

"Overhead?" She shook her head. "No, I've rented an apartment. Not retail space."

"That's right. There are two of them upstairs. I live in one and rent out the other."

"Y-you're my landlord?" she stammered.

"And your neighbor." He grinned. "See, you came to the right place after all."

Right. She was going to be living in a bright-pink building, over a snowboard shop. With Adonis here for a neighbor. Well, she'd said she wanted different. This was about as different from her life in Chicago as she could imagine.

She followed him outside and around the side of the building to a set of stairs in the back. Molly trailed them to the top, where Max unlocked a door that opened onto a long hallway. "Your place is the apartment on the left. I'm right across the hall." He unlocked the door to her apartment and held it open for her.

There were two rooms and a bathroom. The front room was a combination living/dining area with a galley kitchen to the side. She was surprised to see a round cast-iron stove squatting in the corner. "Original to the building," Max said

3 1833 05292 3254

opening the stove door. "Firewood's in a shed out back. Help yourself. It'll keep the place pretty toasty most days."

She walked over to one of two large windows looking out onto a side street. Max came and stood behind her. "You've got a view of a C.B. landmark," he said. He pointed toward a tall, rather plain wooden building. "The two-story outhouse."

"A two-story outhouse?" Was he pulling her leg? Playing the new girl for a fool?

But his expression was perfectly serious. "If you think about it, it makes sense. When the snow gets too deep to dig down to the outhouse, you move the facilities upstairs. It's on the National Register of Historic Places."

Okaaay.

"Bedroom and bathroom are back here…." He showed her the pink-tiled bathroom, with its chain-operated toilet and claw-foot tub, and a bedroom furnished with a massive white iron bed and an oak dresser with a wavy glass mirror. "Are these antiques?" she asked, running her hand along the smooth wood of the dresser. She knew women in Chicago who paid big bucks to furnish rooms in such quaint style.

"Probably." He shrugged. "It all was here when I moved in." He led the way back into the main room. "Phone's on the wall by the kitchen." He pointed to the black plastic princess model mounted on the wall. "We just got satellite last year, so you're in luck." He picked up the remote and aimed it at the television on a stand in the corner opposite the woodstove. "Until last year we had our choice of three stations—and none of them came in well." He switched the TV off. "Of course, you'll probably be too busy to watch much TV, anyway."

"Is the chamber of commerce that busy?" she asked. She

knew Crested Butte was a tourist town, but she hadn't imagined the workload would be so heavy she'd have no leisure time.

"They're busy, but what I meant is there's always something going on in town—parties and things. It's a really happening place."

"Oh. Well, I'm really not much for parties." She had had enough of the social whirlwind back in Chicago. She'd looked forward to evenings that didn't require dressing up, making small talk or smiling until her face hurt. She picked up a red velvet pillow from the sofa and smoothed her hand along the fringe around its edges. "I guess I'm more of a homebody." At least, she wanted the opportunity to be a homebody. How could she figure out what she wanted to do with her life if she didn't try out new things?

"You won't be staying home much around here," Max said. "People around here will find a way to get you involved. You'll see."

Clearly, he was one of those people who couldn't understand that some people preferred to keep a low profile. The whole reason she'd come to this burg on the backside of nowhere was to stay in the background. But really, that was none of his business, was it? She merely nodded politely. "The place looks great," she said. "Thanks."

"It's nice to have a neighbor again," he said, offering her another of his brilliant smiles. She had trouble breathing when he looked at her that way…. *Get a grip,* she ordered herself.

"Let me help you with your stuff," he said.

"Oh, no, that won't be necessary. There really isn't much…."

But he and Molly were already halfway down the hall. Casey followed him out to her car, where he hefted a box of books, and a suitcase from the back. She grabbed the dress bag that had taken up a large portion of the back of the car. It rustled like a sack of dry leaves as she folded it over her arm.

"What's in there?" Max asked as she followed him up the stairs. "Some kind of ball gown or something?"

"Um, something." She absolutely *didn't* want to talk about the contents of the bag with Mr. Gorgeous.

They deposited their loads and returned to the car, where Max grabbed more boxes. "You don't have a bike," he said as she followed him up the stairs again, carrying the ficus.

"No, I don't."

"You'll need one. Don't worry. I'll ask around and find you a good deal."

"Why do I need a bike?" she asked. "Heather said I could walk to work, and I have my car for longer trips."

"Do you want to spend the winter digging your car out of drifts and the summer fighting tourist traffic?" He set the boxes just inside her door, then turned to take the plant from her. "A bike will be much easier. Plus, C.B. has some awesome trails you'll want to check out."

She should have been annoyed that he was so quick to orchestrate her life for her, but these announcements were delivered with such sincerity that she found it hard to object. "Thanks. Maybe I will get a bike. After I've had a chance to settle in more." She could add bike riding to her list of new experiences.

The sound of distant bells floated up to them. "Guess I have a customer," Max said. "I'd better get back to work."

"Yeah. And I'd better start unpacking." She looked around at the stacks of boxes. "Thanks for all your help."

"No problem. See you soon."

It seemed to Casey that Max took some of the air out of

the room when he left. Either that or the altitude was responsible for her light-headedness. She sank onto the sofa and hugged the red velvet pillow to her chest. Dragons, two-story outhouses and pink snowboard shops? She'd said she wanted to live someplace different, but she'd never imagined a place like this existed outside of Lewis Carroll novels. Of course, no one she knew in Chicago could have imagined a place like this, either—and they certainly wouldn't suspect that one of the newest members of the Junior League was now living here. Frankly, she was a little stunned herself.

She carried the dress bag into the bedroom and hung it in the closet. She had to stuff it in, it was so large. Feeling guilty, she carefully lowered the zipper on the bag and admired the confection of ivory satin and lace within. So maybe bringing her wedding dress with her to Crested Butte hadn't been such a great idea. It wasn't as if the dress was much good without a groom. But she hadn't been able to bear the thought of leaving the dress behind. She'd picked it out herself—over her mother's objections—and she knew if she abandoned it her mother would burn it or donate it to charity or something before Casey was even across the state line.

She zipped up the bag and pushed it to the very back of the closet. She had no plans to wear the dress anytime soon, but it made her feel better knowing it was there. The dress was a kind of symbol—proof of the one time in her life that she'd refused to listen to what everyone else wanted her to do and instead had gone after what *she* wanted.

The dress had been the first step. Buying it had proved she could stand up for herself and live her own life.

Coming here to Crested Butte was another big step. Maybe the town wasn't quite what she'd expected, but she'd deal with it. Casey Jernigan, Chicago socialite, was no more. Casey Jernigan, mystery woman, waited in the wings. The part of Casey that wasn't shaking in her shoes at the prospect could hardly wait to see what this new, improved version of herself looked like.

MAX'S FRIEND HAGAN ANSDAR was waiting at the front counter. The tall blonde in the Crested Butte Resort Ski Patrol uniform was rubbing his head and wincing. "You should have a warning sign on that door," he said in a heavy Norwegian accent. "I almost give myself a concussion."

"You need to remember that Victorian doorways weren't built for six-foot-four Norsemen," Max said. He fed another stick of wood into the stove behind the counter and shut the iron door. "Anything exciting happen on patrol today?"

"I met two girls from Austin who are on vacation. One of them broke the binding on her snowboard and I told her I would be happy to repair it for her."

Max shook his head. "It's criminal, the way women fall all over you, just because you wear that uniform and have an accent."

"I told you before. Volunteer for patrol and you can have all the women you want following you around." Hagan grinned.

"Except those aren't the kind of women I want." He held out his hand. "Let me see the binding."

Hagan fished a strip of plastic out of his pocket and handed it over. "How do you know these women aren't the ones you want if you haven't even met them?" he asked.

"Because they're tourists." He examined the piece of binding and frowned. "This has been cut."

"No!" Hagan leaned closer.

Max pointed to the neatly severed edge. "My guess is she decided she wanted the big strong ski-patrol guy to rescue her, so she sliced through the binding strap with a pocketknife."

"That wasn't very smart," Hagan said.

Max grinned. "I don't know. She got what she wanted, didn't she?" He turned to the shelf behind him and pulled down a box. "Here's a new strap. You can install it when you see her again."

"Tonight." Hagan grinned. "She is really hot."

"They all are, buddy. And you're welcome to 'em."

Hagan handed over his credit card and leaned against the counter. "I think tourists are the perfect dates. I see them a few times, then they leave town. No messy relationship problems."

"That's because you don't really have a relationship." Max rang up the sale and returned Hagan's card and the charge slip. "People on vacation aren't really themselves. You don't know these women. You just know how they act away from home."

"That's all I need to know," Hagan said. "And you are one to talk. When was the last time you dated anyone?"

"I go out with women every night," Max said.

Hagan shook his head. "Not groups of friends, men and women. I mean a date. You and one woman. How long?"

Max stuck the charge slip in the cash drawer and slammed it shut. "A while. You know how it is in C.B.—there are more of us than there are of them." In fact, single men outnumbered single women almost two to one.

"And you've already worked your way through all of them." Hagan punched his shoulder. "My way is better. At least until some new women move to town."

"As a matter of fact, someone new has moved to town. She's rented the empty apartment upstairs."

Hagan looked at the ceiling. "Convenient. What's she like?"

"Kind of quiet. But nice."

"Pretty?"

Max nodded. "As soon as word gets around, there'll be a line at her door."

"And you will be first in line, living right across the hall."

Max grinned. "I do have something of an advantage." Although he'd be careful: everything about Casey, from her expensive clothes to her stylish haircut, screamed money and class. In his experience that kind of woman expected a lot from a man.

"Only because I'm excusing myself from that particular competition," Hagan said.

"Yeah—like she'd be interested in a homely guy like you." Max shook his head. "Besides, it's not a competition. I figure, what happens, happens. The point is to go with the flow and have fun." Casey Jernigan might be fun to get to know. If not…well, there were always other women. No need to limit himself unnecessarily.

Hagan laughed. "Good luck to you, my friend." He pocketed the binding strap. "Thanks for fixing me up with this. Mitzi will appreciate it."

"Mitzi? Is she a woman or a poodle?"

Hagan delivered a one-fingered salute and exited, the sleigh bells on the door jangling wildly behind him.

Max checked the display of snowboard bindings and made a note to order more. He could hear Casey moving around upstairs. His new tenant *was* attractive. And though she looked like a city girl, the fact that she'd chosen to move to C.B. said she was up for an adventure.

The thought made him grin. Everyone headed out on an adventure could use a guide. And he just happened to be uniquely qualified to help.

As Casey unpacked, she couldn't help stopping to look out the windows. In addition to the historic outhouse, she had a view of the chiseled mountain the chamber literature had identified as Red Lady. The snow-covered peak took on a crimson glow in the setting sun. The image was almost too beautiful to be real.

She still couldn't believe she was here. Even finding the ad for the job opening had been a sheer stroke of luck. Desperate to get out of Chicago, she'd immediately faxed her résumé, and had been more relieved than overjoyed when she'd gotten the job offer.

So here she was. Tomorrow she'd start work, but until then, she was at a loss for what to do. She picked up the remote control and glanced at the TV, then shook her head. No hiding in her room today. She'd get out and explore her new town. At least she could figure out where to report to work in the morning.

The sunlight was fading fast, and with it the warmth it had brought. Casey zipped her parka to the top and pulled her knit cap lower over her ears, then set off down the sidewalk. She passed a T-shirt shop, an art gallery, half a dozen real-estate offices, several restaurants and a bar, each housed in narrow wooden buildings painted ice-cream pastels.

At the end of the street sat the transit station. A bus painted with bright wildflowers idled by the door. Men, women and children, most dressed in ski clothes, exited the bus and poured into the street, laughing and joking. Vacationers? Or locals lucky enough to live where life was like a vacation every day?

She came to an ice-cream parlor and stopped to pat a shaggy brown-and-white dog waiting patiently out front. Crested Butte was definitely a dog lover's town. Dogs looked out of windows and greeted her from backyards, and half the cars that passed seemed to have four-legged passengers.

A coffee shop beckoned on the corner and Casey quickened her step. A steaming mocha sounded good right now. But her steps slowed as she reached the walkway leading up to the shop. Two men in snowboarding pants, parkas and knit caps were building a moose snow sculpture in the space between the building's front porch and the sidewalk. "What do you think?" one of them asked her. Blond dreadlocks stuck out from beneath his bright green hat. "Are the antlers too small?"

"I don't know," she said. "I've never seen a real moose."

"They're too small." His friend, wearing a red cap over his black hair, frowned at the sculpture. "But we're having a hard time getting them big enough without them falling off."

"Maybe you could use a stick or something as a kind of framework," Casey suggested.

The blonde slapped his friend on the back. "Why didn't you think of that?"

"Why didn't *you* think of it?" the other man asked.

"Because you're supposed to be the brains of this outfit." He grinned at Casey. "I'm the beauty."

"I'm sure you've both impressed her with your looks and intelligence." A woman wearing a bright-pink ski jacket came out of the building and walked down the steps to meet Casey. "I'm Trish Sanders," she said, offering her hand.

"Casey Jernigan. I just moved to town."

"We saw your car pass by a little while ago," the man in the red cap said. He stuck out his hand. "I'm Bryan Perry and my friend here is Zephyr."

She shook hands with both men. "Zephyr?" she asked.

"I'm a musician," Zephyr said, as if that explained everything.

"Welcome to C.B.," Trish said. "What brings you here? Are you into skiing or boarding?"

"Not really. It sounded like an interesting place." Did that strike them as a pretty flimsy reason to move halfway across the country? She pushed the thought away. She'd vowed to leave worrying about what others thought of her behind in Chicago. But lifelong habits were harder to shake than she'd anticipated.

Trish laughed. "It can be pretty interesting. Have you met your landlord yet?"

The question caught Casey off guard. They must have seen her go into the snowboard shop. "Max? Yeah. He helped me move my things upstairs." Though judging by how much everyone already knew about her, she'd bet they knew that, too.

"Be careful around him, girl," Trish said. "Mad Max is the original party boy. Lots of fun, but he's broken a lot of hearts."

Her own heart beat a little faster, remembering Max's killer smile. "Mad Max?"

"Long story." Trish's grin widened. "Nothing to worry about, though. He's a great guy. Just don't make any plans to take him home and show him off to the folks."

The idea almost made Casey laugh. Any man who didn't wear a designer suit and come with a mile-long pedigree was unlikely to meet with her parents' approval. That was only one of the reasons she was glad to be so far away from home. As for Max, well, if she *were* in the market for a boyfriend, she would definitely find him tempting.

She eyed Trish a little more closely. With her long blond hair, blue eyes and high cheekbones, Trish looked like a Scandinavian princess. The kind of woman who'd get a second look from any man. "Do you speak from experience?" she asked.

Trish laughed again. "Nah. I already had a boyfriend when I came here. But I know the type. Ski towns are full of them."

"Don't listen to her," Zephyr said. "She thinks all men are scum."

"Not all of them," Trish said. "But let's face it, most men come to a ski town because they'd rather play than work."

"Then why do most women come here?" Bryan asked.

"Maybe the same thing." She winked at Casey.

"I'm going to go see if I can find some wood or something for the moose antlers," Bryan said. "It was good meeting you, Casey."

"It was nice meeting you, too," she said. "All of you." Her feet were freezing standing here. She stamped them and nodded toward the coffee shop. "Is the coffee any good here?"

"The best in town," Trish said. "Come on in and I'll pour you a cup on the house."

"She only says that because she runs the place," Zephyr said. But he followed the women up the steps and into a small front room that barely had space for three small tables, a combination deli case/front counter and a huge gleaming brass-and-silver espresso machine.

"What'll you have?" Trish said, moving behind the counter.

"A mocha, please," Casey said.

"Whipped cream?" Trish asked, already turning levers on the coffee machine.

"Of course."

"I'll have one of those, too," Zephyr said.

"You have to pay," Trish said.

He grinned. "Put it on my tab."

Trish rolled her eyes, but pulled a second cup from the stack by the machine. "So where are you from, Casey?" she asked.

"Illinois."

"Where in Illinois?" Zephyr asked.

"Um…Chicago." She watched his face carefully. Would her name ring a bell?

"No kidding." He shook his head. "Never been there."

She relaxed a little. She didn't know why she was worried. People out here probably didn't care about the society pages in the Chicago paper. And *she* wasn't going to care about them anymore, either. "I'm going to be working at the chamber of commerce," she said. "But I bet you already knew that."

"You probably think we're nosy, but C.B. is still a small town," Trish said. "A new person moving in is big news."

"Especially a new, single female." Zephyr removed the top from a glass jar of biscotti and helped himself, dodging Trish's hand slap.

"Oh?" Casey asked. "Why is that?"

Trish's eyes widened. "You didn't know? I thought maybe that was one reason you came out here."

"Know what?"

"Single men outnumber women two to one in ski towns," Zephyr said.

"Military bases and Alaska are the only places you're likely to find a better ratio," Trish said. "Of course, like I said before, that depends on your definition of eligible bachelor." She angled a look at Zephyr.

"What?" he asked, brushing crumbs from the front of his sweater. "Chicks dig musicians."

"Tourist chicks, maybe," Trish said. "Those of us who know you better aren't so sure." She handed Casey a steaming cup topped with a mound of whipped cream.

Zephyr grinned. "You only say that because you want my body."

"Like I want cellulite and chapped lips," Trish said.

Casey sipped her coffee and kept quiet. The drink was sweet and rich and warmed her through. But more warming still was the feeling of being accepted so quickly by these strangers. All her life she'd heard about small town residents' views of outsiders. Maybe the locals-versus-tourists mentality in Crested Butte negated all that.

"You should stop by the Eldo tonight," Trish said.

Casey vaguely remembered passing a bar by that name. "What's going on at the Eldo?" she asked.

"Just the regular Sunday Night Soiree," Zephyr said. "One last chance to party before the workweek begins."

"All your neighbors will be there and it'll be a good opportunity to meet them," Trish said.

Max hadn't been kidding when he'd said it was impossible to stay uninvolved in C.B. She half expected if she said no, people would come and drag her from her room. But honestly, everyone was so friendly she didn't really want to refuse. And the Sunday Night Soiree didn't sound anything like the boring social events she'd endured too often in Chicago. "Thanks," she said. "Maybe I will."

She was feeling better about making this move. The people she'd met so far made her feel that being a little bit different wasn't a bad thing. Who knew, she might even find what she needed in this place to slay a few personal dragons of her own.

Chapter Two

The Eldo was a long narrow room occupying the upper floor of a building at one end of Elk Avenue. The place was packed, every table and barstool occupied by young men and women, the crowd spilling out onto the balcony that overlooked the street. Despite the frigid temperatures, the balcony was full and patrons cheerfully called down to friends and passersby on the street below.

"Is it always like this?" Casey asked Trish as the two women squeezed past a group of pool players on their way to the table Bryan and Zephyr had saved for them. The table was near the small stage where two guitar players and a drummer played enthusiastically if not well.

"Mmm. Sometimes it's worse." Trish maneuvered past two men who were arm wrestling and plopped into a chair.

"I ordered us a pitcher," Bryan said, his voice raised to be heard above the band. He grinned at Casey. "I'll bet there aren't many places like this in Chicago."

"None that I've visited," she said truthfully. Her mother would faint it she knew Casey was here now, drinking beer poured from a pitcher in a place she would no doubt have called a dive. Casey smiled and took a long sip of beer. The idea of unsettling her mother pleased her.

One of the arm wrestlers looked up from the struggle and spotted Casey and immediately released his hold on his competitor. He stood and came over to them. "Hi," he said, grinning at Casey. "Wanna dance?"

She looked around at the packed bar. As far as she could tell, there wasn't five square feet of free space anywhere. "There's nowhere to dance," she said.

"Sure there is." His grin widened. "We'd just have to stand really close to each other."

"Um, no thanks."

"Maybe some other time, Chris." Trish gently pushed the man away. "Casey just got here. Let her relax a little before she gets into the swing of things."

Bryan grinned. "It's already happening."

"What's happening?" Casey asked.

"I told you a single woman in this town was big news," Trish said. "Now that you've been noticed, you'd better be prepared."

"Prepared for what?"

But Trish didn't have time to answer, as a waitress staggered toward them with a tray loaded with drinks. She set the tray down heavily in front of Casey. "These are for you," she said.

"For me?" Casey stared, dumbfounded, at the half a dozen glasses—everything from bottled beer to a margarita to some drink that featured a number of cherries and a frilly pink paper umbrella. "I couldn't drink all this. I'd be ill."

"We'll help." Zephyr plucked a bottle of beer from the tray.

Trish picked up the pink umbrella drink and grinned. "Everyone just wants to make you feel welcome."

Casey nodded and took another sip from the glass of beer she'd already started. "I don't know what to say. It's a little...overwhelming." Coming to town, she had had a vague idea that because no one here knew her or her family, she would be able to fade into the background. Her past experiences being the center of attention had made her wary of the spotlight.

"Enjoy it while you can," Trish said. "Pretty soon you'll be just another local and no one will look at you twice."

"Oh, I wouldn't say that," Bryan said thoughtfully.

Trish elbowed him and he gave her a mock-wounded look. But Casey's attention was quickly distracted by a trio of men in ski-patroller uniforms who were headed her way. "Hello," they chorused.

Casey blinked, sure she'd fallen asleep and been sucked into a bizarre dream. "You're Casey, aren't you?" one of the men—a sunburned guy with thinning brown hair—said.

She nodded. "And you are?"

"I'm Mike. This is Scott and Eric."

She nodded. "Nice to meet you, I'm sure."

The three found chairs from somewhere and pulled them up to the table with the arm wrestlers. Soon Casey was peppered with questions about where she was from, what brought her to Crested Butte, did she want to have dinner, dance, have a drink, go hiking, skiing, biking, skating, et cetera, et cetera.

She felt dizzy and dazed and after a while stopped answering them, letting Trish fill in the details she knew. More drinks arrived at the table. More people crowded around them. The band stopped playing and they joined the group around the table also. At some point someone turned on a stereo or jukebox and the three ski patrollers took it upon themselves to serenade Casey with a very bad rendition of the Grateful Dead's "Casey Jones." She didn't quite get the connection, but then, nothing about this town really made sense.

About that time she looked up and saw Max watching her from across the room. She was so grateful to see a familiar face—and one that didn't seem determined to impress her, woo her or find out everything about her—that she could have wept.

His eyes locked on hers and he frowned, then started toward her. He waded through the crush of people, easily shoving aside chairs and stepping over the tangle of out-stretched legs and feet. "Are you guys trying to drive Casey out of town her first day here?" he asked the three ski patrollers.

"We were just providing a little entertainment now that the band was done," one of the men—Eric?—said.

Max shook his head. "From what I heard, there wasn't anything entertaining about it." He offered Casey his hand. "If you're ready to leave, I'll walk you home."

A chorus of groans and catcalls greeted this offer, rising in crescendo when Casey let him pull her out of her chair. "It was nice meeting all of you," she said. "But I really am exhausted."

She followed Max through the crowd to the door. They didn't speak until they'd descended to street level. It was snowing, tiny flakes gently drifting down like powdered sugar shaken from a jar. The chill night air hit like a slap in the face, reviving her. She drew her parka more tightly around her and gave Max a grateful look. "Thanks for coming to my rescue," she said.

He nodded. "You looked a little overwhelmed in there."

"It was all a little…much." They began walking slowly down the deserted sidewalk, sidestepping patches of ice.

"Take it as a compliment," he said. "Everyone wants to welcome you to town."

"I guess I hadn't expected my arrival to be such a big deal."

"Hey, it's not like it's the end of the world." He patted her shoulder. His hand was heavy, comforting. She tried to ignore the tickle of desire that fluttered in her stomach at his touch. Max was only being friendly.

Right, the warning voice in her head—which might have been her conscience—said. *And grizzly bears only want to be friendly, too. No danger there at all.*

She forced a smile to her face and a lightness to her voice. "I'm sure everyone will get tired of me soon enough."

"I guess this is a big change for you, being from a big city and all," Max said. "It's a lot easier to be anonymous there."

She laughed at the irony of his words. As the daughter of the mayor's chief aide, she'd never felt particularly anonymous. From the time she could toddle, her parents had been hauling her to campaign rallies, charitable balls and other prominent social functions. Her picture had appeared in countless editions of Chicago papers, usually in the society column. Her mother dutifully saved each one, delighting in the fact that her daughter was so popular. For a time, Casey had enjoyed it herself, but after a while the constant scrutiny had chafed. The older she got, the more the public seemed to expect from her, until she began to feel her life wasn't her own.

Which was partly why she was in Crested Butte. As much of a cliché as it was, she'd come here to find herself. To rediscover the Casey she'd lost somewhere along the way.

"What's so funny?" Max asked.

"Nothing." She shook her head. "Nothing at all." She tilted her head up and let the snowflakes kiss her cheeks. Away from the din of the Eldo, the street was silent except for the crunch of their feet on the fresh snow. She felt more at peace than she had in months.

"What are your plans for tomorrow?"

Max's question startled her out of her reverie. She glanced

at him, curious but cautious. "I start work tomorrow. Then...I don't know. I thought I might buy groceries." She shrugged. "Nothing exciting."

"After work, why don't you let me show you around." He wasn't looking at her, but off to one side, his voice deliberately casual.

"Are you asking me out on a date?"

He shook his head. "A date? No."

"No?" She couldn't keep a note of disappointment from her voice.

"No. A date would be dinner or a movie or something like that. I just thought—if you're going to be working for the chamber of commerce, you need to know the area, so you can direct tourists and stuff. I need to run up to the resort sometime tomorrow to trade out some stock with a snowboard shop up there. I thought you could ride with me and check things out." He shrugged. "Just as a friend."

That certainly sounded nonthreatening enough. "Okay. That sounds good."

"Good. We'll talk more tomorrow."

She was surprised to find they were already at the foot of the steps leading up to the apartments. "Are you coming up?" she asked.

"No. I think I'll go back to the Eldo for a while."

"Thanks again for everything," she said.

"Sure. No problem." He shoved his hands in his coat pockets and took a step back. "Good night."

"Good night."

She climbed the steps, but stopped on the landing outside the door to look back. Max was striding away from her down the street, his shoulders hunched against the cold. He made a romantic figure, snow falling around him.

Of course, when he'd left her at her door to go back to the bar it hadn't been terribly romantic, but then, what did she expect from a man whose nickname was Mad Max?

Not that she was interested in romance, anyway. She'd come here looking for a change. A chance to figure out what she wanted to do with her life. Romance, she knew from experience, could mess things up.

Max had offered to be her friend; the prospect intrigued her. A woman starting over needed new friends and what woman wouldn't want a good-looking man like Max on her side?

BEFORE OPENING THE SHOP Monday morning, Max and Molly walked to the post office to collect the mail. Normally, Molly would have run and played in the fresh snow, but at the moment she was too pregnant to do much but plod along, looking up at Max from time to time with the perpetual smile goldens always wear. "It won't be long now, girl," he told her. "Our place will be puppy central." Fortunately, a number of Molly's future offspring were already spoken for. Then she was off to the vet to make sure this didn't happen again.

He passed the Eldo and thought of Casey. Who was he kidding? He'd thought of little else since he'd left her last night. She definitely wasn't the party girl or outdoorsy-type the town usually attracted. He was trying to figure out exactly how she'd ended up in C.B. When he'd spotted her at the bar last night, she'd had a desperate look in her eyes. The look of someone who was involved in something she wasn't quite sure of.

Which set off more than a few warning bells in his head. He'd had his share of dealings with confused women before— women who wanted him to straighten out their lives for them. Or, worse, ones who thought *his* life needed straightening.

He reached the post office and gathered the mail. After discarding a stack of junk mail and flyers, he was left with a snowboarding magazine, two bills and two letters addressed to Casey.

That was fast, he thought. After all, she'd only arrived yesterday. But he supposed she'd given out the address as soon as she'd leased the apartment and the letters had been mailed before she even left Chicago.

He studied the return addresses. One was from Mr. and Mrs. Charles Jernigan. Her parents?

The other was from a Paul Rittinghouse. Max frowned. Brother? Cousin?

Boyfriend?

His jaw tightened at the thought and he shoved the letters into his pocket. On one hand, why should it surprise him that a woman like Casey would have a boyfriend? She was pretty and smart with a nice personality.

On the other hand, if she *did* have a steady boyfriend, why would she move so far away from him?

Another mystery to add to the growing list about Casey. She was a city girl who wasn't particularly interested in skiing or snowboarding or any of the other activities that led people to abandon all and move to the mountains. She obviously had been uncomfortable as the center of attention last night, but at the same time she wasn't painfully shy or socially inept.

No doubt about it, Casey intrigued him. She might be too complicated for girlfriend material, but there wasn't anything wrong with getting to know her better.

Strictly as a friend.

CASEY TOLD HERSELF she shouldn't be surprised when she walked into work Monday morning and the first person she saw was a woman wearing a red feather boa and carrying a sequined toilet plunger. Less than twenty-four hours in Crested Butte had taught her that this was a place where she should expect the unexpected.

She was thrown a little off guard, however, when the woman in the boa introduced herself as Heather Allison— Casey's new boss. "I'm so glad to see you," Heather said after they'd exchanged introductions. "We have so much to do and I'm positively thrilled to have some help."

"I'm happy to be here," Casey said, trying not to stare at the rest of Heather's outfit, which included a purple velvet cape and a crown cut from aluminum beer cans.

"Hold this a minute and I'll get the employment paperwork you need to fill out," Heather said, handing Casey the plunger. She went to a large wooden desk and began rifling through piles of paper on the top. "I know I put them somewhere…." She tossed aside a yellow rubber duck, a pair of maracas and strings of Mardi Gras beads. "Aha. Here they are." She waved a sheaf of papers.

Casey could contain herself no longer. "What's with the plunger?" she asked. "And the crown?"

Heather laughed. "You've arrived just in time for Flauschink—our annual end-of-ski-season festival."

"Flauschink?" Casey tried out the odd-sounding word.

"Literally, *flushing,* as in flushing out winter. Hence the plunger."

"So everyone carries these around for the festival?" Casey eyed the sequined toilet accessory.

"Not everyone. Only the king and queen. I was trying out this year's queen's costume when you walked in." Heather plucked the crown off her head and placed it on Casey's. "I think the costume committee outdid themselves this year."

Casey watched while Heather divested herself of the royal robes. Underneath the purple velvet she wore a sensible black pantsuit. "When is Flauschink and what happens during the festival?" Casey asked.

"It's next weekend. Closing weekend for the ski resort and the last gasp for winter tourists. As for what happens, here's a schedule." She thrust a flyer at Casey.

Casey read down the list of activities, eyes widening. "Polka ball, crowning of king and queen, ski race, parade, concert…" She looked up. "That's a lot to plan for."

"So you see why I'm so glad you're here." She took the plunger and crown and stowed them in an empty file drawer. "You can fill out that paperwork later. Right now you would save my life if you could call this list of bands and confirm they're going to be here to play next weekend. I've found it pays to follow up. You know musicians."

Casey was happy to take a seat at the desk and get to work. Work felt normal—something she hadn't experienced much of since leaving Chicago.

After Casey confirmed with all the musicians, Heather asked her to proof some ads for the summer Wildflower Festival. "It's our biggest draw of the year," Heather explained. "So we do a huge advertising push in newspapers and magazines."

"So after Flauschink, we start getting ready for the Wildflower Festival?"

"Oh, before the Wildflower Festival we have Poo Fest and Bike Week, then the Wildflower Festival, the Arts and Film Festival and Vinotok—the fall festival." Heather ticked the events off on her fingers. "Then it's time for ski season and all the winter activities—which are too many to name right now."

"Poo fest?" Casey asked. "You mean shampoo?"

"No. Dog poo. The snow melts and all the trails and side-walks need to be cleaned up. A few years ago someone came up with the idea for the Poo Fest. There are games and prizes for the person or team that picks up the most pounds of poo."

"You're kidding." This had to be another attempt to pull one over on the new gal.

Heather shook her head. "I swear I'm not. It's a lot of fun. And a great way to get everyone to pitch in to clean up."

Casey shook her head. Was there anything folks here wouldn't celebrate?

Mid-morning, the men began showing up.

First was a young man with bright red hair. He came in clutching a brown paper bag. "Is Casey here?" he asked, looking past Heather toward Casey's desk in the back.

"Wanted to be the first, did you, Jerry?" Heather said.

Jerry's cheeks matched his hair. He moved past Heather to Casey's desk and set the bag on top. "Hi, I'm Jerry," he said. "Welcome to Crested Butte."

"Uh, hi, Jerry." Casey eyed him warily.

"I brought you sort of a welcome gift," he said, nodding to the bag.

"Thanks." She studied the plain brown bag. "Um, what is it?"

"Moose poop."

"Okay." Another joke on the newcomer? How was she supposed to take this?

She sent a frantic look at Heather, who marched over and snatched up the bag. "No wonder you're still single, you dolt," Heather said. She opened the bag and fished out a round brown patty and bit into it.

"Don't worry," she said in answer to Casey's horrified look. "It's chocolate. A local specialty." She offered the bag to Casey. "Try one. They're delicious."

Casey fished out a smaller patty and sampled it. "It *is* good!" she said, relieved. Belatedly, she remembered the man who'd given her this gift and offered him a smile. "Thanks."

"You're welcome." He shoved his hands in his pockets and took a step back. "Well, I guess I'll be seeing you around."

Jerry was scarcely out the door before a burly man with a black beard walked in. He marched up to the women and offered his hand. "Bill Whitmore," he said. "Welcome to C.B."

"Hi, Bill," Casey said.

"I thought you might like to have lunch," Bill said.

Casey glanced at the clock. "It's only 10:30."

"Well, sure. Not now. I could come back later."

"Casey's going to have lunch with me." Heather pushed Bill toward the door. "And now she has to work."

But in between meeting Gary, Eric and Anders, Casey wasn't able to accomplish much. "What is going on?" she asked after yet another man left the chamber office.

"It'll get better tomorrow," Heather said. "You'll probably have met them all by then."

"Met who? Are they some sort of official welcoming committee?"

Heather laughed. "I suppose you could look at it that way. They're all single guys stopping by to check you out."

Casey sat back in her chair, dumbfounded. "I thought I'd met them all at the Eldo last night."

"Single women—especially young, pretty ones—definitely have an advantage here in C.B.," Heather said. "You can have your pick of men. Only problem is, a lot of them aren't worth picking."

Casey fiddled with a pencil, turning it over and over in her hand. "I'm not sure I like that. It makes me feel—I don't know—like fresh meat in the tiger cage at the zoo."

"Don't let it get to you," Heather said. "These guys are harmless. Just lonely. They won't hassle you. And you'll never have to eat dinner alone unless you want to."

"Does that mean you don't eat many dinners alone?" Casey asked.

Heather snorted. "I eat dinner with my twelve-year-old daughter, which makes me immune to a lot of the attention you're getting."

"But you're not that much older than me," Casey said. "And you're gorgeous." Heather had curly brown hair and a classic hourglass figure. "Men should be lining up to see you, not me."

"I'm thirty-one," Heather said. "So, no, not that old. But too long in the tooth for a lot of these ski bums, and having an almost-teenager in the house scares off most of the rest of them." She sighed. "It's okay, though. There's always hope, that's what I say. And hey, I can live vicariously through you. That's why you were hired, you know?"

"Because I'm single?"

"No, but the job did come open because my last assistant got married and moved to Denver."

"Did she marry one of the local men?"

"Nope. Snagged herself a tourist. A nice businessman from the big city. So I put out the call for a new assistant and here you are."

Casey nodded. "Is there anything else I need to know about this place? I mean, besides the dearth of single women and the abundance of weird festivals? Any unusual local customs? Places or people to avoid?"

Heather laughed and checked her watch. "It's almost noon, what say we grab a bite to eat? I'll fill you in on everything you need to know."

Chapter Three

Heather locked up the office then she and Casey headed down Elk Avenue to the Teocalli Tamale. The interior of the little shop was warm after the chill outside and the air was fragrant with the smell of onions and green chili. "Hello, Patti. Ben." Heather greeted the woman behind the order window and another diner. "This is Casey Jernigan, my new assistant."

"Hey, Casey." Patti nodded.

"What'll you have?" Heather asked. She indicated the menu posted on the wall to their right. "It's all good."

Casey ordered a chicken burrito and iced tea, while Heather opted for a taco salad and a diet soda. Patti assembled their meals right away and the two women carried their trays to one of the tables.

"Ben Romney." The distinguished man with thinning brown hair and kind blue eyes came over to them and offered his hand. "Nice to meet you."

"Ben is the local orthopedist," Heather explained. "He stays busy patching up tourists and locals alike."

"How is Emma?" Ben asked.

Heather frowned. "At the moment she hates my guts because I refused to let her get her belly button pierced."

"She'll get over it," Ben said.

"Yeah. Maybe in another five or six years." Heather looked at Casey across the table. "Last week she was upset because I wouldn't let her dye her hair purple. Before that she pitched a fit because I refused to let her spend spring break in Mexico with a bunch of kids I don't know."

"You're doing a good job with her," Ben said. "She'll appreciate it one of these days."

"Here's your order, Ben." Patti walked over and handed him a white paper bag.

"Wish I could visit with you ladies more, but I've got to get back to work. I've got a young man waiting who will probably need surgery on his knee."

"Skiing accident?" Casey asked.

Ben shook his head. "Fell off his roof shoveling snow. Happens all the time."

Sure it does, Casey thought. *Why am I even surprised?* "He seems nice," she said after Ben had left them.

"Yeah." Heather salted her salad. "You should try the green chili sometime. It's to die for."

"I'll do that."

They were silent a moment, eating, then turned their attention to the boisterous group crowding in the door of the restaurant.

"Be still my heart," Heather said, clutching Casey's arm.

"What?" Then she recognized Max in the group of men. He had his back to her, busy removing his jacket and the long scarf wound around his neck. Her heart beat a little faster, seeing him. He probably had that effect on everyone.

He turned around and saw her and his grin lit his whole face. "Hi, Casey. How's your first day at work?"

"It's going great," she said.

"Hello, Hagan." Heather's voice was pitched two notes higher than usual. Casey turned to look at her boss and held back a grin of her own at the sight of Heather's flushed cheeks and bright eyes. So Max wasn't the man who made Heather's heart race.

"Hello, Heather." A tall blond with a soft accent nodded to the women on his way to a table on the other side of the room.

"Hi, Heather," Max said. "How's it going?"

"Okay." Heather turned in her chair to look after Hagan. "You two are welcome to join us for lunch," she said.

"Thanks, but Hagan isn't good company today," Max said. "He's been unlucky in love." He winked and moved past them.

Heather faced forward again and rested her chin in her hand, lips turned down in a pout. "I know all about unlucky in love. He's probably just mad because some snow bunny stood him up last night."

"Is he a skier?" Casey asked.

"Ski patrol." Heather sighed. "You should see him in his uniform. No wonder half the women on the mountain are literally falling at his feet."

Casey's own record with men wasn't stellar enough that she felt qualified to give advice to Heather. She returned her attention to her food, but all the while she was aware of a certain big man seated in the corner of the room.

She was looking forward to their promised trip up the mountain to the resort later this afternoon, but she didn't know what to make of her obvious attraction to Max. Maybe it was merely a combination of his good looks and his willingness to help her out of a jam last night. He was a friendly guy, but she had no business reading anything more into it than that. After all, history had proved she was a lousy judge of what constituted romance.

"So just how big was Mitzi's boyfriend?" Max asked as he and Hagan stood at the front counter.

"Very big." Hagan rubbed his jaw, which was taking on a purple tinge. "Good thing I turned or he would have broken my jaw."

"Funny how she forgot to mention this boyfriend."

"I suspect she was trying to make him jealous." Hagan studied the menu and shrugged. "It happens."

"Yeah, but games like that can get a man killed. Or at least crippled."

"Worse, I'm out twenty dollars for the binding strap." He scowled. "Women. Never trust them."

"That's what you get for dating strangers."

"And as I said before, you are not one to be giving advice about dating." He looked up as Patti approached. "Would you go out with him?" He pointed to Max.

Patti raised one eyebrow. "What? Is he your broker or something?"

"Ignore him," Max said. "He took a punch to the jaw and it rattled his brains. Bring us a couple of specials."

"Poaching on someone else's territory, Hagan?" Patti asked.

Hagan straightened. "Why do you say that?"

Patti shook her head and began assembling their burritos.

"Why did she say that?" Hagan asked Max.

"You have a reputation, dude."

"Hmmph. At least they don't call me Mad Max."

"A name I happen to like." He frowned at his friend. He should have taken Heather up on her offer to join her and Casey for lunch. The conversation was bound to be better. He turned away. "Holler when the food gets here."

Hagan grunted and went back to brooding. Max walked

over to Heather and Casey's table and took a seat. "What's new at the chamber of commerce?" he asked.

"Casey got the full treatment this morning," Heather said. "Jerry Rydell brought her moose poop and Bill Whitmore asked her to lunch."

"Isn't Bill dating Marcy over at the library?" Max asked.

Heather shrugged. "Guess he's keeping his options open."

Max grinned at Casey. "I'm sure you made a good impression on all of them." He ignored the pinch in his gut that might be jealousy. After all, he'd been the first to welcome her to town, and living across the hall from her, it was only natural he'd feel a little territorial.

"I don't want to make an impression on any of them." Casey shifted in her chair. "I'm sure they're very nice guys, but I didn't come to town on some kind of man hunt."

"Enjoy it while you can," Heather said. "After you've been here a while you'll be just another local like me. Yesterday's news."

"Did she tell you a bunch of lifties serenaded her last night?" Max grinned.

"No!" Heather laughed. "I'll bet that was a riot."

"Sounded like a bunch of raccoons fighting over leftovers," Max said.

Casey joined in the laughter. "It was pretty terrible," she said. "Max ended up rescuing me and taking me home."

"Any woman who drives halfway across the country by herself with only a houseplant for company doesn't need rescuing," he said. "I figured you were worn out from your trip and didn't need the hassle of dealing with those guys anymore."

He'd been standing by the bar, making fun of the singing when he'd locked eyes with her across the room. She'd looked exhausted and more than a little lost in the midst of the raucous crowd. What man wouldn't have stepped in to help her?

"Well, I appreciate it, anyway," Casey said. She rearranged her silverware, avoiding his eyes. Which was a real shame. She had beautiful eyes. The gray of a stormy sky.

He reached into his pocket and pulled out the letters that had come for her this morning. "These were in the mail for you," he said.

She took the letters, frowning when she read the address on the first one—the one from Mr. and Mrs. Charles Jernigan. When she got to the one from Paul Rittinghouse she positively glowered. "You don't look too thrilled with mail from home," he said.

She glanced up at him, her cheeks flushed, then folded the envelopes in half and stuffed them into her pocket. "I'm surprised, that's all. I mean, I just got here."

"They must have been mailed before you left," he said.

"You're probably right." Her expression brightened, but he had the impression the look was forced. "Heather has been telling me about the Flauschink Polka Ball," she said.

"I was explaining to her she needs to come up with a costume," Heather said.

"And I've been trying to explain to her I'm not really much for fancy parties," she said. She'd attended enough overdone celebrations in Chicago to last a lifetime.

"I wouldn't call the Polka Ball *fancy*," Max said. "It's mostly just fun."

"Your costume will have to be something simple," Heather said. "We've only got a week. And I don't think anything in my closet will fit her."

"What about that ball gown or whatever it is in your

closet?" Max asked. The thing had taken up half her car, like one of those hoop-skirted costumes from *Gone with the Wind* or something.

"No." She shook her head, her cheeks a deep pink. "That wouldn't be appropriate at all."

Heather gave Max a questioning look. He shrugged. Whatever was in that bag, Casey clearly didn't want to talk about it and he wasn't going to push it.

"Why do I have to have a costume?" Casey asked. "Couldn't I stay home?"

"And miss one of the best parties of the year?" Max asked.

"You haven't lived until you've heard the polka version of 'Bohemian Rhapsody,'" Heather said. "Besides, we'll need you there to help sell tickets and things like that."

"Maybe I'll wear what I have on and go as a normal person," Casey said. "I can wear a sign around my neck that says Endangered Species."

Max laughed. "That's pretty good. But the whole point is to shake you out of normal person mode. It'll be good for you." She obviously had a sense of humor, but there was a certain tension about her, as if she were always reining herself in.

"Do you have a red dress?" Heather asked.

"Not entirely red, no. Why?"

"Does it have some red in it?"

She nodded. "But why do you want to know?"

Heather turned to Max. "I've got red heels and red fishnet hose she can borrow. And my red feather boa. She can go as Miss Scarlet."

"Miss Scarlet?"

"From the board game Clue. Ben Romney came last year as Colonel Mustard and we all said it was a shame we didn't have a Miss Scarlet, too."

"What are *you* coming to the party as?" Casey asked Max.

He grinned. "You'll have to show up and find out."

"Last year he was Mr. Disco, in orange bell-bottoms and a rainbow Afro." Heather laughed. "Add a clown nose and big shoes and you could use the same outfit as a clown costume."

"I promise you will be astounded and amazed by my costume this year," Max said. He'd outdone himself, if he did say so.

"Your food's getting cold," Hagan called.

"We have to get back to work, anyway." Heather stood and Casey rose also.

"See you later, neighbor," Max said.

The smile she gave him made him warm clear-through, setting off warning bells in his brain. He did his best to ignore them. He and Casey would be friends, that's all. He didn't have any intention of taking things any further. Why ruin a good friendship with something as messy as romance?

THAT AFTERNOON, Casey waited until Heather was involved in a lengthy phone call before she slipped the letters out of her pocket. She opened the one from her parents first, already pretty sure of what it would say.

As she'd expected, the letter in turns scolded her for being so *foolish and irresponsible,* pleaded with her to *come to her senses and return home* and reminded her how disappointed they were that she had embarrassed them so in front of all their friends.

Of course, that was what was most important, wasn't it? The impression she gave to all their friends. Never mind what she might be feeling. What she might want. Over the years she'd tried in various ways to tell her parents that she didn't want the kind of public acclaim and popularity they craved, but she could never make them understand.

And worse, they'd almost succeeded in convincing her that she was wrong, that *of course* she was *supposed* to lead the kind of life they'd planned out for her—the good marriage to a prominent member of society, the memberships in the Junior League, the League of Women Voters, the Chicago Art Project, et cetera, the house in Madison Park or the Gold Coast and a vacation home on Martha's Vineyard. Shopping at all the right stores, eating at all the right restaurants, knowing all the right people.

She'd almost believed them. Until the morning she woke up in a panic and realized that if she didn't do something soon—something drastic—she'd be trapped forever in a life she'd never wanted.

She glanced over and saw that Heather was still on the phone. She dropped the letter from her parents, along with the envelope, into the shredder and watched with relief as the missive was reduced to paper ribbons.

But when she looked at the second letter, her relief vanished, replaced by sheer dread. Why had Paul written her? Obviously, her parents had given him her address here. Possibly they'd even encouraged him to try to talk some sense into her. Because, of course, anything she did that went against their wishes was senseless.

She stared at the envelope, at the neat, clipped handwriting. As upright and proper as the man himself.

Not that there was anything wrong with Paul, she reminded herself. He was a perfectly nice man. Good-looking. Rich. The perfect boyfriend.

Except he hadn't been perfect for her and she couldn't make anyone believe that. Not even, apparently, Paul.

She sat there, hand poised to tear open the envelope. But really, what could he say that she wanted to hear? He wasn't going to make her think differently. He wasn't going to make her go back.

Quickly, before she changed her mind, she leaned over and fed the letter, unopened, to the shredder.

Then she sat back with a sigh of relief, feeling as if she'd narrowly avoided a collision with a Mack truck.

Oddly enough, it was the same feeling she'd had when she'd made the decision to come here to Crested Butte. Everyone else thought she was crazy, but right now this was better than any sanity she'd previously known.

WHEN SHE AND MAX MET UP later that afternoon, Casey was surprised to learn they were taking the bus up to Crested Butte Mountain resort. "I'd have to dig out my Jeep to use it," Max said, carrying a box full of miscellaneous snowboard parts to the bus stop in front of the chamber building. "Besides, the bus is free—the tourist tax dollars at work."

Casey wasn't about to admit she'd never taken public transportation before, much less something like this funky painted bus full of tourists. As the aide to the mayor, her father supported public transportation, though he didn't feel that required him or his family to use it. Casey had traveled by private car, taxi or even limousine service.

"The bus is a great idea," she said, as she followed him into the vehicle. This one was decorated with a scene of the mountains in summer, covered in wildflowers. She settled onto the seat beside Max and looked around at their fellow passengers: a mom and dad and their three children bundled up in ski jackets and knit caps, a group of teenagers similarly dressed, a young couple holding hands and an older man dressed in a chef's uniform, obviously on his way to work at one of the resort hotels.

The bus pulled away from the stop and Casey turned her attention to Max. "Where are you taking the box?"

"George Taylor's, right at the base of the lifts. I didn't need this stuff and they did, so rather than me send it back and them ordering more, we're doing a trade."

"So you have a good relationship with your competition."

He gave her a *duh* look. "Pretty much all the business owners up here get along. No reason not to. There's room for all of us."

In fifteen minutes the bus dropped them off in front of a soaring wood-and-steel building. "New condos," Max said. "They sell out as fast as they can build them, so they keep building more."

Casey turned to take in the tall buildings that rose on all sides. "It certainly looks different here than it does in town," she said. Rough-hewn stone, oversize timbers and artful use of rusted metal gave the buildings the feel of a Bavarian village—a very tall, very modern Bavarian village. Groups of smiling people, some carrying skis or snowboards, all bundled in colorful parkas, made their way along the walkways between the buildings and the rows of shops that sold ski equipment, clothing and souvenirs.

"The resort is really growing," Max said as they started up the sidewalk. "The condos have changed the look of the mountain, but that's progress. The tourists pay the bills and at least we've kept it confined to the mountain."

They came to an icy stretch of pavement and Max took her arm. The chivalrous gesture—or maybe it was the masculine strength of the hand supporting her—sent a pleasant warmth through her. "Thanks," she said.

"Sure." She half hoped he'd keep hold of her, but as soon as they were clear of the ice, he released her.

Past the condos, they could see the slopes, the ski lift silent, empty chairs swinging in the cold wind. "Do you ski or snowboard?" Max asked.

"I've skied some, on vacations with my parents or friends." But those trips had really been more about wearing the right fashions and making the right connections than the actual skiing.

"Now that you're living here, you'll have the chance to get really good if you want," he said.

She glanced at him. "Are you really good?"

"I do all right. I have to test out the equipment to sell it, you know."

They entered the snowboard shop. After the night chill, the interior of the shop felt almost too warm. A young woman in a pink baby-doll T-shirt layered over a white thermal underwear top waved at them. "Hey, Max. George is in the back."

A bearded young man in a leather apron hailed them from the back of the shop. "Hey, Max." He took the box from him. "Thanks for bringing these in. Sue's got a check for you."

"No problem. This is Casey. She's new in town—works at the chamber."

"Welcome to town." George shook hands with her, then turned back to Max. "Have you seen those new mono-skis I just got in?"

"No. Let me check them out."

While the men talked equipment, Casey wandered to a rack of clothing and began thumbing through the jackets, pants and knit tops. She'd definitely need to add to her wardrobe of casual clothes. Most of the suits and dresses she'd brought with her were too formal even to wear to work. Even business was a more casual affair in C.B. than it had been in Chicago.

Max collected his check and Casey, then they emerged

once more into the cold. A few snowflakes swirled around them. "Let's grab a bite to eat," Max said. "The Avalanche has good food." He nodded to a restaurant across the way.

Casey started to ask if including dinner now made this a date, but refrained. And once they were seated in the restaurant, she had to admit this was like no date she'd ever been on. Max seemed to know everyone and it took fifteen minutes to order their meal because they were constantly interrupted by people. Everyone who stopped by learned that Casey was the new employee of the chamber of commerce. "I'm showing her around, helping her get familiar with the area," Max said.

"Cool," his friends said. Or "Welcome to C.B." No knowing looks or winks were exchanged. Nothing to suggest this was anything more than two friends enjoying a meal.

But it wasn't exactly like a meal with one of her girl-friends, either. Max ordered what she and her friends had always called "man pizzas"—pies piled with meat and every other topping available. "Is that okay with you?" he asked be-latedly.

She shrugged and unfolded her napkin across her lap. "Sure." When in Rome and all that.

Their pizza arrived and the traffic around their table died down. "Do you know how many snowboarders it takes to change a lightbulb?" Max asked between bites of pizza.

"No, how many?"

"Three. One to change the bulb, one to videotape it and one to say 'Awesome, dude!'"

She hadn't expected this and struggled to keep Diet Coke from coming out her nose as she laughed.

"How many ski instructors does it take to change a light-bulb?" Max continued.

She shook her head, laughing.

"Six. One to change the bulb and five others to say 'Nice turn.' 'Nice turn.' 'Nice turn.'"

She groaned. "That's bad."

"One more and I promise I'll stop." He helped himself to another slice. "What are a snowboarder's last words?"

She shook her head. "I can't even guess."

"Dude! Watch this!"

She dissolved into giggles again. It wasn't that the jokes were so funny, but that he looked so delighted to be sharing them with her. Their eyes met and she felt the definite sizzle of attraction.

She looked away and fussed with the napkin in her lap. Now this definitely didn't feel like any date she'd had before. None of the men she went out with acted silly or went out of their way to amuse her. And she'd never experienced this sudden shift from laughter to lust. Was it the altitude, the novelty of her surroundings or something else entirely?

They finished eating, Max consuming the lion's share, then walked back to the bus stop. It had stopped snowing again, but the wind had picked up. The icy chill seemed to slice right through Casey's coat. She wrapped her arms across her chest and shivered. "I can't believe it's this cold in April," she said.

"Nights can be cold here into the summer," Max said. He put his arm around her and pulled her close in a hug. "Let me warm you up."

It was a friendly gesture, but an intimate one, too. It felt good, his strong arm encircling her, the warmth from his body radiating to hers. She raised her eyes to meet his and found him studying her intently. "What is it?" she asked.

"You're not like most of the women I've met up here," he said, his voice soft and low.

"Is that a bad thing?"

"No. I like it. I mean, I like you. You're...your own person." Their eyes remained locked and she wondered if he would kiss her. Part of her thought she wouldn't be able to stand it if he didn't—and part of her wanted to run away if he did.

But after a moment, he withdrew his arms. "Here comes the bus," he said.

They found a seat on the bus and he avoided looking at her again. Instead, he directed his attention out the window. "There are some great trails up there," he said, indicating a snowy forest-service road. "Good fishing in the lakes, too."

"I don't fish," she said. "But I suppose some of the people who come into the chamber do. I'll keep that in mind."

"That paved path you can barely see is the Hike and Bike trail," he said, indicating a trail on their left. "It goes all the way from Crested Butte up to the resort."

"I'll have to try it sometime." She kept her eyes on him, but he continued to avoid her gaze. She wondered if that moment of intimacy back at the bus stop had unnerved him even more than it had unsettled her.

When they reached Crested Butte, they climbed off the bus and walked up the street in silence. Neither said anything until they were in the hallway to their apartments. "Thanks for showing me around tonight," she said.

"Anytime." His earlier easiness had returned. "And if you need anything in your apartment or whatever, let me know."

"The apartment's fine," she said. "Very nice."

"Good night." He nodded and turned toward his door.

She stared after him, amusement warring with confusion. For someone Trish swore was a ladies' man, Max certainly hadn't made any moves tonight. He'd been exactly what she needed—a good friend.

Of course, she thought, as she unlocked her door and went inside, what she *needed* and what she *wanted* weren't necessarily the same thing. She'd have to be careful to not let her suddenly-wide-awake libido get the better of her common sense. Better to get a handle on this new life she was creating for herself before she wandered off into the dangerous territory of a new love interest.

Though when she was ready to head off into that particular wilderness, a mountain man like Max might be the perfect guide.

Chapter Four

Casey decided that if someone combined a Halloween party with a square dance and a junior prom, the result would be the Flauschink Polka Ball. It was definitely nothing like the fancy balls she'd endured in Chicago, she thought as she and Heather joined the crush of people at the entrance to the Eldo while the oompah beat of "Roll Out the Barrel" poured from the open doors.

Heather wore a black leotard and tights, and had fastened two large white dots to her torso. "I'm a domino," she explained. "The two-spot."

Casey had succumbed to Heather's badgering and dressed as Miss Scarlet, complete with a red feathered headdress, red boa, red fishnet stockings and stiletto heels, and a long black cigarette holder unearthed from the prop department of the community theater troupe. Since Casey didn't smoke, Heather had stuck a bubble wand in the end of the holder. She'd handed Casey a plastic bottle of bubble solution. "You'll be a hit," she declared.

Okay, so it was kind of fun blowing bubbles over the heads of the assorted clowns, cowboys, devils, angels, snowmen and the other characters that converged inside the Eldo.

Casey had scarcely gotten her bearings when a man wearing a red long underwear top, rough canvas pants, suspenders and a bushy black beard grabbed her hand. "Let's dance," he said.

Casey resisted. "I don't know how to polka," she protested.

"Then it's time you learned." The man—she decided he was supposed to be a miner—swept her onto the dance floor and led her in a somewhat controlled gallop across the room.

"Who are you?" she shouted over the insistent polka beat.

"Bill Whitmore. We met at the chamber."

Of course. She'd mistaken the beard for a fake, but now realized he'd let it go untrimmed to add to the authenticity of his outfit. "Someone told me you had a girlfriend," she said as they started back across the room.

"That's okay. She's dancing with someone else."

When the song ended and Bill released her, she was gasping for breath. "Guess you're not used to the altitude," Bill said, delivering her to a table shared by Heather, Trish, Bryan and Zephyr.

"Guess not," she wheezed, dropping into a chair. If she'd had the breath, she might have added that she wasn't used to being dragged around at a gallop, while wearing high heels, either.

"We ordered you a drink." Heather pushed a plastic cup toward her.

Casey had drained half the cup before she realized the fruit punch was heavily spiked. "Maybe I'd better stick to water," she said, pushing the cup away.

"We've got that, too." Trish handed her a bottle.

Casey twisted off the cap and searched the crowd for familiar faces. She'd half expected Max to offer to ride with her over to the Eldo, since walking even that short distance in heels was out of the question, but she hadn't seen him since he'd locked up his shop that afternoon.

"He's not here yet," Heather said.

"Who?" Casey asked.

"Max. That is who you were looking for, wasn't it?"

She hoped everyone would mistake the flush on her cheeks for the effects of her dancing. "I'm curious what his costume might be," she said.

"There's Dr. Ben." Trish, dressed as a flapper in a white silk minidress and rolled stockings, waved at a man in a familiar beer-can crown and purple cape.

As he approached, the good doctor saluted them with his plunger/scepter, which also doubled as a holder for a can of beer. "You're the Flauschink King!" Casey exclaimed.

"Yes, I do have that dubious honor." He turned to Heather. "You're a very lovely…uh…what exactly are you?"

"I'm a domino," she said, exasperated.

"Where's your queen?" Zephyr asked. He'd added a silver lamé jacket to his usual baggy jeans and introduced himself as a rock star.

Ben looked around, then a smile broke out. "Here she comes now." He waved and Patti, the waitress at the Teocalli Tamale, glided over. She wore a tie-dyed T-shirt and ripped jeans beneath her royal robes, and tie-dyed streamers decorated her scepter.

"Dig the tie-dye, your majesty," Zephyr said, giving her a thumbs up.

"Thanks." Patti curtsied.

"Anybody seen Max?" Ben asked.

They shook their heads. "We're all waiting to see his costume," Bryan said. He was dressed as a chimney sweep, in top hat and tails, carrying a broom. "Do you know what it is?"

Ben shook his head. "It was all top secret."

"Has anyone seen Hagan?" Heather asked. "What's he wearing?"

"Just look for the crowd of women," Trish said. "I heard he was repeating his Thor costume, it went over so well last year."

"Thor?" Casey asked.

"Picture Hagan in leather boots, tight leather pants, fur vest and horned helmet," Heather said. She fanned herself. "He looked awesome."

"Didn't he carry a big cardboard thunder bolt or something?" Ben asked.

"He'd have to get a new thunderbolt this year," Patti said. "Someone sat on last year's."

Casey sipped her water and listened to their recollections of previous years' costume winners. "Jerry Rydell came as a match one year," Ben said. "With his red hair it was perfect."

"Marcy Wagner came as a bunch of grapes one year," Heather remembered. "She wore purple balloons fastened all over her body. It looked great until people started popping her balloons."

Zephyr nodded. "All she had on underneath was a slip. She tried to talk old man Cafferty, who was king that year, into lending her his robe, but he wouldn't do it. She ended up wearing one of the tablecloths the rest of the night."

A movement near the door caught Casey's attention and she sat up straighter. She couldn't keep back a smile as a familiar figure came into view. "There's Max," she said.

Heather turned to look. "Oh, my," she said. "That might even beat out Hagan for the sexiest getup."

Sexy was right. Max wore a tattered black leather jacket over a black T-shirt, fingerless leather gloves, tight black leather pants, tall black motorcycle boots and a studded gun belt. Heavy stubble added to the dark and dangerous look.

"He's *the* Mad Max," Casey said, trying—and failing—to suppress the heat that curled through her as he strode toward them. His gaze locked on hers and she felt she might melt into a puddle right there in her chair. It was one thing to acknowledge that her neighbor/landlord was an attractive man. It was another to see him this way, radiating masculinity and raw sex appeal.

"You'd give Mel Gibson a run for his money," Heather said when Max reached their table.

"You look great," Casey said, unable to take her eyes from him.

"You look pretty great yourself, Miss Scarlet." He picked up the cigarette holder that was lying on the table in front of her and eyed it quizzically. "What's this stuck in the end?"

"Show him," Heather said.

Feeling a little silly, Casey picked up the holder, dipped it in the jar of soap solution and blew a long string of bubbles. They bobbed in the air around her head, iridescent in the light of the disco ball suspended over them.

Max laughed, then turned to Ben and Patti and executed a deep bow. "Your majesties."

"I always thought your nickname was from the movie," Ben said. "But I take it you haven't worn this costume before."

"His nickname has nothing to do with the movie," Trish said.

"Don't tell that story," Max said. He looked pained.

"Well she *has* to tell it now," Heather said. She looked at Casey. "Besides, you should know what kind of a man you have for a neighbor."

Max groaned. "I can't believe you people still remember this."

"How could we forget?" Trish leaned forward, her face

alight with barely contained glee. "One day about six years ago, right after Max opened his shop there on Elk Avenue, this tourist couple came to his place and wanted to rent bicycles. They had a dog with them and Max asked what they were going to do with the dog while they rode. They said they were going to leave it in their car."

"And Max told them it was too hot in July to leave a dog locked in a car." Heather took up the story. "He wouldn't rent the bikes to them until they promised to take the dog back to their hotel and leave it there."

"Except he didn't really trust them, so he made note of their car and after a little bit he took a ride up to the bike trail-heads until he found the vehicle," Trish said.

"And the dog was in the car," Ben said. "Figures."

Casey kept her eyes on Max. His mouth was tightened to a thin line, his expression made all the more forbidding by his costume. "What happened?" she asked.

"I broke their window with a rock and took the dog back to my shop with me," he said.

Ben choked on his drink. "You broke their window?"

"It was the only way to get the dog out. He was already panting hard when I got there."

"What did they do?" Casey asked.

"They came after me, said they were going to file charges, demanded the dog back. I told them I'd pay to replace their window, but they couldn't have the dog."

"Of course the story spread all over town," Trish said. "Somebody said you didn't want to mess with a mad Max and the name stuck."

"Is that how you got Molly?" Casey asked.

He shook his head. "I just got Molly a couple of months ago. Pete—the dog I rescued—died last fall. He was fourteen.

Hagan found Molly behind one of the restaurants up on the mountain and brought her to me. I told him I didn't really want another dog, but he insisted." He grinned. "Hagan's a hard man to say no to."

"*I* wouldn't say no to him," Heather leaned over and whispered to Casey.

"Her Royal Highness and I have to leave," Ben said. He offered his arm to Patti. "Duty calls. The paper wants us for pictures."

"I'd better go, too." Zephyr slid out of the booth. "The band said I could sit in with them."

"Can you play polka music on an electric guitar?" Trish asked.

"*I* can," Zephyr said, and left with Ben and Patti.

The three bumped into Hagan as they were leaving. "Hello, everyone," Hagan said, taking the seat next to Heather that Zephyr had vacated.

Casey had to admit he was breathtaking, in a muscular, primitive way. Heather couldn't stop staring at him, her eyes glassy.

"I don't know if it's safe being around this much testosterone," Trish said. She looked at Bryan. "Want to dance?"

"Sure."

They left and Max slid into the booth next to Casey. His thigh touched hers and she discovered she was having trouble breathing. "You okay?" he asked. "You look a little flushed."

"Must have been the spiked punch I had earlier." She took a long swallow of water.

"Be careful with the alcohol at this altitude," he said. "It can really sneak up on you if you're not used to it."

Could she blame the altitude for the sudden rush she felt for the man next to her?

"Want to dance, Hagan?" Heather asked.

Hagan shook his head. "No, thanks. These fur boots aren't made for polka."

"Why polka music?" Casey asked.

Heather shrugged. "Why not?"

"It's a Crested Butte thing," Max said. "We sort of excel around here at being different for the sake of being different."

"I've noticed." She couldn't decide if that meant she'd fit right in or not.

"Where is everyone going on vacation for mud season?" Heather asked.

"Mud season?" Casey frowned. Was this another weird celebration, like Poo Fest?

"In May, the snow melts," Hagan explained. "Everything turns to mud. Most people try to leave town to get away from the mess."

"I just got here, so I won't be leaving town," Casey said.

"Emma and I are going to Disney World," Heather said. "At first Emma said she was too old for that kid stuff, but when I told her I didn't mind riding the rides by myself while she waited back at the hotel, she decided it might be fun after all."

"I'm going to Canada," Hagan said. "Fly-fishing."

"What about you, Max?" Heather asked. "Where are you going?"

"I'm staying here."

"Why do that?" Hagan asked. "No one else will be here. Except Casey." He grinned. "Then again…"

"I'm staying because Molly's due to have her puppies and I don't want to leave her." He turned to Casey. "She was pregnant when I got her. Probably why she was dumped in the first place."

Casey nodded. She was still trying to wrap her mind

around the idea of a whole town going on vacation in May. "Does everyone really leave town for the month?" she asked.

"Most people try to get away at least part of the time," Heather said. "The winter tourists are gone and the summer visitors haven't arrived yet. The weather is as lousy as it ever gets here and everyone is sick to death of seeing everybody else. So it makes sense."

It did make sense, Casey realized, in that skewed way of looking at things that was as natural for people here as breathing the thin air.

"I guess this means I'll be holding down the fort at the chamber by myself while you're gone," she said.

"Don't worry, it'll be really slow," Heather said. "If you feel like leaving, the answering machine will get whatever calls come in."

"I don't know where I'd go," she said.

"You can always help me do inventory if you get really bored," Max said.

Boring was not the first word that came to mind when she considered the possibility of hours spent alone with Max. "I might take you up on that offer," she said. If nothing else, she'd learn a little about bicycles and snowboards—and about Mad Max himself.

MAX REALLY HATED that Trish had told everyone that story about how he got his nickname. Whenever women heard it, they invariably got all moony over him. Hagan would have used that to his advantage, but worshipful looks only made Max nervous. Tell most women you'd rescued an animal and they started picturing you with babies and little kids. A man could go from fun, sexy date material to potential perfect mate in the time it took to tell that one story.

He didn't want to be anybody's mate, perfect or otherwise. His older brother and sister had both married well and were busy producing perfect grandchildren for his parents, so Max had no obligation there. All he had to do was look at their idea of domestic bliss to know he wanted no part of such a scene.

He studied Casey out of the corner of his eye, trying to decide if she showed any signs of mooniness. When her face didn't go all soft and her eyes dreamy, he relaxed a little. She struck him as the type who didn't rush into anything, be it romance or the local social scene. Which made him all the more curious why she'd pulled up stakes in Illinois and headed for Crested Butte. She'd said she was looking for a change, but why?

"Would you like to dance?" he asked.

She shook her head. "I don't think I like polka dancing much."

"We don't have to polka. I can ask them to play a slow song."

She shook her head. "That's okay."

"Go on and dance with the man." Heather nudged her shoulder.

Casey glanced at Heather, then back at Max. "Okay."

"Be right back." He slid out of the booth and made his way to the stage where the band had set up. He beckoned to Zephyr. "Play something slow," he said. "Casey and I want to dance and she doesn't like polka."

Zephyr grinned. "Coming right up."

By the time Max had made his way back to the booth the band had segued into a slow, jazzy number. He held out his hand to Casey. "They're playing our song."

He liked the way she felt in his arms. Her red dress was

silky beneath his palm at her back and he fought the temptation to slide his hand down lower. "Why did you change your mind about dancing with me?" he asked.

"I knew Heather wanted to be alone with Hagan."

He frowned. "She's wasting her time with him."

"Why do you say that?" She tilted her head to one side and looked him in the eye, her tone challenging. "Heather's a wonderful woman. And she's really pretty."

"*And* she's way too settled for Hagan. He likes playing the field."

"Trish says most of the men in town are that way."

She didn't sound disapproving, but maybe he didn't yet know her well enough to tell. "I think the lifestyle here—the vacation atmosphere, all the outdoor activities—does tend to attract people who are more mobile and active," he said. "The kind of people who aren't really ready to settle down."

She nodded. "I guess so."

"Isn't that why you're here?" he asked.

"I didn't really know much about all the activities or the lifestyle," she said. "I was looking for a change."

Her gaze slid away from his.

"Uh-huh," he said. "A change from what?"

She stiffened in his arms. "Just…a change."

They brushed against another couple and he pulled her closer, enjoying the way she fit against him. "Crested Butte is definitely different," he said. "So tell me about your life in Chicago. What did you do there?"

She hesitated, as if she was about to refuse to answer his question, but then she said, "I worked for an advertising agency. Nothing special."

"Do you have family there?"

Another hesitation. "My parents are there."

Curiouser and curiouser. "What happened to make you decide to move way out here?"

Her eyes met his again. "I don't want to talk about it."

Her look, so intense and pleading, hit him in the gut. He tightened his hold on her and fought the crazy urge to demand to know who or what had hurt her. After all, he hardly knew her. She was just another beautiful woman—one he might or might not like to know better.

Strike that. He definitely wanted to know her better. He wanted a free and easy friendship. No complications. Hagan would have laughed and told him women by their very nature were complicated. Max sensed Casey might be more complicated than most. He wasn't sure it was a good idea to get involved with someone who made him this light-headed and confused, but it might already be too late.

Chapter Five

The end of April brought warmer temperatures and melting snow. Crested Butte's dirt streets became quagmires. Businesses closed and people left town in a steady caravan. Even the chamber phones all but stopped ringing, leaving Casey plenty of time to organize the files, read every brochure in the racks lining the walls and wonder again what she was doing here. Crested Butte wasn't the money-and-status-fueled high society she'd fled, but was it really where she belonged?

One morning in the first week of May, Max stopped by the chamber office to deliver her mail. Her cell phone bill, a couple of magazines, the Junior League newsletter and yet another letter from Paul. Her parents had had sense enough to stop writing when she didn't answer them, but Paul wrote faithfully every week. Curiosity had driven her to open a couple of the letters, but they were both the same: calm assertions that if she would only return home and talk with him, he was sure they could sort everything out, followed by reminders of how much she had embarrassed and disappointed everyone who cared about her, winding up with a promise of his forgiveness for this uncharacteristic lack of judgment on her part if she would only return home.

Nothing about undying love or wanting to be with her or even questions as to what might be bothering her. Nothing to make her want to read any more of his letters. So now she held firm to her policy of feeding them straight to the shredder, which she did now with the newest missive, while Max looked on, one eyebrow arched in question.

"This Paul guy must have really pissed you off," he said.

"Mmm." Originally, Paul had done nothing in particular to upset her, but his continued refusal to accept that she was an intelligent adult, capable of taking charge of her own life, annoyed her greatly.

She studied the cover of one of the magazines. *Glamour.* She'd bet not many women in C.B. bothered to subscribe. Not that the women here didn't take care with their appearance, but when the climate dictated sturdy clothes and shoes that wouldn't be ruined by mud and the nearest store selling haute couture was miles away over steep mountain passes in either Denver or Aspen, the importance of high fashion tended to fade.

"So who is this Paul guy who keeps writing to you?" Max perched on the edge of her desk.

She eyed him cautiously. Like most of the people she'd met in C.B., Max was so open and friendly he probably couldn't imagine a person might have things about herself she wanted to hide. "What if I told you I didn't want to talk about him?" she asked.

"I'm guessing he's a boyfriend. Someone you left behind in Chicago who's trying to talk you into coming home."

She squirmed. She was pretty sure he hadn't read any of the letters; they'd all been delivered to her tightly sealed. "That's about it," she said. She was aware of his eyes on her, waiting for her to elaborate. Instead, she changed the subject.

"Where's Molly?" she asked. "Why isn't she with you today?"

"I left her behind. I think it's getting pretty close to time for the puppies to arrive."

"I hope she'll be okay." In the few weeks she'd been here, she'd grown to really like the sweet yellow dog.

"She'll be fine. Though I might ask for your help with the puppies."

"My help? What could I do?" She had never had a pet of any kind, much less a newborn puppy. Her mother objected to the mess animals made.

"I might need someone to keep an eye on Molly and the pups while I'm out at night or something. Just in case they needed anything."

She relaxed a little. "I could probably do that."

He looked around the chamber office. "Looks like things are pretty slow here," he said. "What do you do all day?"

"I've organized all the files and fliers, planned out the ad campaign for the Wildflower Festival and read all the back issues of the chamber magazine," she said. She had spent most of this morning arranging all the brochures in alphabetical order, then rearranging them alphabetically by subject matter—all the outfitters together, followed by lodging, restaurants, et cetera. She had been debating organizing them by color into attractive patterns when Max had showed up.

"You need a break," he said. He stood. "Leave the phone on the answering machine and come with me."

The idea of going off alone with him sent a small thrill through her. And surely they would be alone—almost no one they knew was still in town. "Why? What do you have in mind?"

"It's time we got you that bike," he said. "And maybe did a little exploring."

MAX TOOK CASEY to his shop, where she followed him into the back room where the rentals from the previous season were stored.

"What are you doing with all these bikes?" she asked, looking around at the bikes suspended from the ceiling and lined up along the walls.

"Some of them will go on sale next month," he said, eyeing them critically, looking for the perfect ride for Casey. "Others will go into the rental pool." He reached into the jumble of handlebars and hauled out a purple-and-silver mountain bike. "Try this one," he said, wheeling it into a cleared area.

Casey eyed it skeptically. "I haven't ridden since I was ten."

"It's not something you forget. Come on, try it out."

She shrugged and swung her leg over the frame. He grinned. She looked right at home there already. He took out a wrench and adjusted the seat. "Perfect."

She studied the bent handlebars bristling with brake and gear cables. "Don't you have anything less complicated?"

"Sure, we could get you a real townie bike." He nodded toward an old-fashioned Schwinn with a white wicker basket suspended between the handlebars and wire panniers draped across the back fender. "Practical for around town, but hard going on the mountain trails." He patted the purple bike. "This baby gives you the best of both worlds."

"How much?" she asked.

"Borrow it for a while, see if you like it. Otherwise it will go into my rental fleet."

"I don't know…."

"Come on, let's try it out."

He hung a closed sign on the shop and wheeled his own bike out of the back. The day was crisp enough to require a light jacket, but a hint of summer warmth tempered the air. The first wildflowers were beginning to bloom along the margins of vacant lots, hinting at the colorful bounty to come with summer.

"Let's try out the path up to the resort," he said, mounting up and pedaling the few short blocks to the paved trail. They pedaled across a wooden bridge over Coal Creek, across the wetlands, past the horse pasture, winding up to the condos and luxury homes clustered around the ski area. He showed Casey how to shift gears and soon she was huffing and puffing along behind him. He stopped at the top of a small rise to allow her to catch up.

"I thought I was in shape," she said. "This is killing me."

"It's the altitude," he said. "Plus, you're using muscles you don't normally use. It will get better, I promise." She looked great, cheeks flushed from exertion, hair tousled by the wind.

But then, she always looked great. The other night at dinner he'd found himself noticing the way her hair curled around to cup the sides of her face, noting her long, delicate fingers. When she'd complained of the cold, he'd welcomed the excuse to hold her close, then realized the danger of the move as his body responded to her warmth and feminine curves. He'd come really close to kissing her then.

And a kiss itself probably wouldn't have been so bad. He got the feeling she wouldn't object. But he didn't want to take things too fast. He thought of Casey the way Hagan thought of the dynamite charges the ski patrollers used to set off avalanches within the ski resort boundaries: handled properly, the explosives gave a man exactly the results he wanted. Try to rush things and everything could blow up in his face.

"One thing at least," Casey said, unzipping her jacket, "the exercise warmed me up."

"If you want to take off your jacket, I'll put it in my pack."

"Good idea."

While they shed their jackets and stuffed them into Max's pack, she looked around them, at the mountains rising up on all sides, the red and gray rock broken by patches of dark green firs and the paler green of aspen. "This is gorgeous," she said.

"It was even better before all the homes went up." He pointed to a house under construction nearby, massive log beams and broad expanses of windows dominating a ridge top. "These places sell for a million bucks, easy. And half of them are empty most of the time. They're vacation homes, used only a few weeks a year."

She looked at him, a curious expression on her face. "Maybe they think it's so beautiful here they want a little piece of it, even if they can only see it a few times a year."

"Maybe. I'd rather see the land stay vacant, but nobody asked me. I guess that's progress for you."

They walked the bikes up another steep rise until they were at the edge of Crested Butte Ski Resort. Patches of snow still dotted the slopes, but the lifts sat silent. "In a few weeks they reopen the lift," Max said. "People can ride to the top of the mountain and hike or bike down. There are some beautiful views up there. Sometimes you can see marmots and other wildlife up there, too."

"I'd like to go up there," she said.

"I'll take you. It'll be fun."

She smiled. "Everything is fun for you, isn't it?"

"Why not? Beats a life of drudgery."

"I suppose…but maybe the drudgery makes the fun even more enjoyable."

"Now you sound like my mother," he said as they continued walking.

"Ouch! Why do you say that?" she asked.

"I'm the black sheep of the family. I've got a brother and sister who are every parent's dream—Ivy League educations, successful, well married. The kind of people who never make mistakes." Whereas he'd fumbled his way through life, making more than his share of blunders.

"How did you end up in Crested Butte?" she asked.

"I came here with some buddies during Christmas break one year and never went home. I stayed with friends and worked a lot of different jobs." He laughed. "The saying around here is that people in C.B. like jobs so much we all have three or four of them. Most of the work is part-time—in restaurants and retail shops. I was lucky that when the guy who owned the snowboard shop where I worked decided to move back east, he let me buy the place for a good price." He held out his arms. "And here I am." His life was nothing like the one his parents had dreamed of for him, but he was all the more proud of it because it was his own.

"Where was home before?" she asked.

"Connecticut. My dad owns his own business." He glanced at her. "I think the idea was that I'd join him one day. Instead, my brother and sister are doing the honors. They love it, so everything worked out."

"I guess most fathers want their sons to follow in their footsteps," she said.

"I tell them they ought to be happy I'm self-supporting, healthy and doing exactly what I want in life." There had been a time when even that was in doubt—back when he was struggling through school, always the problem child.

"Yes, that's the way it should be."

"What about your parents?" he asked, anxious to shift the focus from his own troubled past. "What do they think about you moving out here?"

She frowned. "They weren't very happy about it."

"Because they wanted you closer to home? Or for some other reason?"

"A lot of reasons." She shrugged. "I guess you could say I didn't turn out exactly the way they wanted, either." She flashed a smile that hit him like a punch in the gut. That and her next words had him off balance for a moment. "I'm a black sheep, too. That's one thing you and I have in common."

He returned the smile. "I knew we'd get along great the moment I met you," he said.

Her eyes widened. "You did?"

"Yeah, I did." It was odd, really. His reactions to women were usually pretty predictable: he'd notice how they looked; he'd figure out how high-maintenance they were then he'd assess the possibilities of getting to be friends with them.

Only with Casey had all of the above taken a backseat to the idea that he just really *liked* her. Being with her made him feel good. Simple. And yet, pretty complicated, too.

"Come on." He mounted his bike again. "We've rested enough. Let's try something a little more challenging." He rode to the end of the block and turned onto a narrow dirt trail that led down a slope and disappeared into the woods behind a housing development. Not much of a trail, but he needed to burn off some of the jitteriness all this talk of families and thoughts about his feelings for Casey had generated.

He heard her rattling along behind him and grinned. Now that she had a bike, he could show her all kinds of great places. He'd help this city girl discover her inner mountain woman. He sped up, reveling in the feel of the wind in his hair, the muscles of his thighs knotting as he pumped the pedals.

He heard the slide of bike tires on loose gravel about the same time Casey screamed. He looked back in time to see her somersault over the handlebars and tumble down the slope, the bike jouncing after her. He braked hard, almost falling himself. But he managed to regain control and bring the bike to a stop. He tossed it aside and ran toward Casey, who was sitting up now, cradling her right knee.

"What is it?" he asked, dropping to his knees beside her. The sight of her ashy face made him sick to his stomach. What if she'd broken a bone or something? "Where does it hurt?"

"My knee." She moved her hands to reveal a bloody scrape embedded with gravel.

Max looked at the knee. He'd seen a lot worse, though this probably hurt plenty. "Anything else?" he asked. "Any broken bones? Did you hit your head?"

"No. I'm okay." She flexed her arms and straightened her left leg to demonstrate.

"Hang on, I've got a first-aid kit on my bike." He ran back to his bike and retrieved the plastic case from the zippered pouch beneath the seat and raced back to her. "What happened?" he asked as he opened the kit.

"I slid on the gravel and I guess I panicked and hit the brake too hard."

He tore open an alcohol wipe. "This doesn't look too bad. You'll be sore for a couple of days, but you'll be all right."

She sucked in her breath as he dabbed at the wound. "Maybe I'm not cut out for this," she said. "Maybe I should get a townie bike and stick to paved streets."

"Don't say that." With a pair of tweezers from the medical kit, he began picking gravel from the wound, then used a water bottle to flush it, his hand shaped to her calf to steady the knee.

"I shouldn't have taken you on such a steep route," he said. What had he been thinking? He hadn't been, obviously, as his dad often liked to point out. "Not without at least giving you a few pointers for riding off-road." She had very nice legs—smooth and shapely and decidedly feminine. He was getting turned on working on her, feelings that were complicated further by the guilt he felt over getting her into this mess. He smeared antibiotic ointment on the wound, then stuck a gauze pad over it, taping it loosely in place. "Keep it clean and when you get home, leave it open to the air as much as possible."

"Yes, doctor," she said, her tone teasing. "But how am I going to get home?"

He sat back on his heels. If this had been a male friend of his, Max probably would have suggested he suck it up and ride back to town. But Casey definitely wasn't a guy, and he could see she was already tired from the ride out here. "We'll walk back. Take it slow. After all, we're not in a hurry to get anywhere in particular."

She looked doubtful, but nodded. "Okay."

He helped her to her feet, then retrieved her bike from where it had landed. "Is it okay?" she called.

"It's fine." He set the bike upright. "These mountain bikes are pretty tough."

"Tougher than their riders, obviously."

She accepted the bike and wheeled it up the trail ahead of him. She had an obvious limp, and a streak of dirt down one arm, but he decided she would make it back to town okay. And next time they went riding together, he'd choose a better trail.

And there *would* be a next time. He'd see to it. As long as she didn't hold this screwup against him. He wanted the chance to prove to her that he could do a few things right.

CASEY WAS NOT A COMPLAINER and she tried not to be one now. But wrestling a heavy bike up a steep slope while sharp pain radiated from her knee with every step was not her idea of a pleasant afternoon. Still, she grit her teeth and marshaled on, not wanting Max to think she was a complete wuss.

She was breathing hard and grimacing by the time they reached the street again. Max helped her pull the bike up the last steep incline and patted her shoulder in a comforting gesture. "You're doing great," he said. "And it probably doesn't feel like it now, but walking will be good for your knee. It'll keep it from stiffening up."

"I've never been all that keen on doing unpleasant things that are good for me," she said.

"Just think of it as part of that drudgery that makes the fun times better."

She stuck her tongue out at him and he laughed. He had a wonderful laugh—deep and melodious.

He wasn't like any other man she'd met. He was so easy to be with, maybe because he was so easy with himself. He had no expectations as to how she should behave, what she should wear or say.

"You don't ever worry about impressing anyone, do you?" she asked.

He glanced at her. "Why should I? Or is that a sarcastic comment on my appearance?" He raked one hand through his shaggy hair.

She shook her head. "No comment. It's one of the things I like about you. You are what you are and you don't care what people think." Something she'd struggled with for as long as she could remember—that internal battle between personal desire and public expectation.

"I guess you could say that's my philosophy in life," he said. "People should be authentic."

She nodded. He made it sound so easy. "But how do you know what's authentic for you?" she asked. "I can think of lots of things I *don't* want, but I'm not sure I know what I do want." One of the reasons she'd come to C.B. was to try to sort out that puzzle.

He looked thoughtful. "Part of it goes back to when I was growing up. I don't mean I had a horrible childhood or anything—my family was great. They still are. But I never felt like I fit in with them." He glanced at her, as if weighing his next words. "Everyone else in my family is really smart and really successful. Everything comes easy to them. I wasn't anything like my brother or sister and my parents couldn't understand it. I mean, I was supposed to go to college, get a degree, come home and help Dad run the family business, marry a local girl and raise a family. Instead, I left school and moved thousands of miles away. I guess you could say I like my independence."

Independence. It was a heady word. Something she hadn't experienced much of until she'd left Chicago. She'd never done anything truly on her own prior to coming here. She'd attended the school her mother had gone to, as it had been expected she would, joined the clubs her parents favored. Her job in marketing was at a firm owned by a family friend. Even Paul had been introduced to her by her mother.

And now she was here. Living by herself, working in a job she'd gotten by herself. Walking with a man who believed that making his own decisions and living his own life was a wonderful thing.

"Why are you looking at me that way?" he asked.

She blinked. "Why am I looking at you what way?"

"As if you're not sure whether to measure me for a strait-jacket or kiss me."

She smiled, and leaned toward him. "Why don't we start with the kiss?"

He stared at her a moment, blue eyes unblinking, startled. She saw the moment the decision was made but scarcely had the time to register this when he closed the gap between them.

When their lips touched, she realized she'd been anticipating this moment all day—or maybe even since they'd met. He slid his hand around her waist, bringing her closer, angling his mouth to more fully cover hers. She felt the scrape of his beard stubble against her cheek and inhaled the wood-smoke and washed-cotton aroma that clung to him. The sun warmed the top of her head and her bare arms and though they stood in the middle of an open valley, they might have been the only two people in the world.

It was one of those rare times in her life that had no other agenda. She was unhurried, focused on the feel of his lips, the taste of his tongue and the pleasure to be found in the embrace of someone who made her feel more alive to every sensation simply by his presence.

When they broke apart at last, she was light-headed and amazed at her own recklessness.

"That was nice," he said, his eyes bright with a definite heat.

Nice didn't begin to describe the sensations that sparked through her. She rubbed her arms, chilled without his hands on them, and took a deep breath. "It was," she agreed, then had to turn away, breathless at her own impulsiveness. What was she getting into with this man who was so different from anyone else she'd known and so exactly what she needed in her life right now?

IN MAX'S EXPERIENCE, first kisses were all about experimenting. Another step in getting to know a woman better. A pleasant sensory exploration. Was she tentative or assertive? Passionate or reserved? Giving her all or holding back? The thrill of new discovery mingled with the uncertainty of uncharted territory. There was a certain awkwardness to first kisses that couldn't be avoided.

With Casey, he had felt all of this and more. In some ways, the moment his lips touched hers, it was as if he'd been kissing her for years—or, more precisely, as if all those other kisses had been mere rehearsals for this one. His whole body had been attuned to her. He'd been physically turned on, to be sure, but more than that, he'd felt an emotional connection with Casey.

The knowledge had shaken him at first, but now that they were almost back to the shop and he'd had time to process things, he saw it as one more sign that Casey understood him. She saw the authentic him—the free-spirited black sheep—and she liked what she saw.

The more he thought about it, the better he felt. Maybe, at last, he'd found that perfect woman. The one who could be his friend as well as his lover, without a lot of heavy expectations to mire them down.

As they approached the shop, he stifled a groan. A familiar figure was slouched against his front door. "Is that Zephyr?" Casey asked.

"I don't know anyone else who'd be wearing tie-dyed painter's pants and a sweater that looks like it was rejected by the Goodwill bin."

At their approach, Zephyr straightened and walked to meet them. "Hey! If I'd known you were going for a ride, I would have joined you."

Max started to say something about three being a crowd, but Casey spoke first. "I thought you'd left town with everybody else," she said.

"Nah, I've been house-sitting up on the mountain. One of those big vacation homes." He shoved his hands deep in the pockets of his baggy pants. "I was getting kind of lonely, though, thought I'd come down and see what was shakin' in town."

"I'd love to stay and talk, but I'd better get upstairs and see to my knee," she said. She turned to Max. "What should I do with the bike?"

"Leave it here. I'll carry it up for you later."

"Thanks." Her eyes met his and she felt a jolt in the pit of her stomach. "I had a great time today. Except for the fall."

"Yeah. Me, too."

He kept his eyes on her until she disappeared around the side of the building. When he looked at Zephyr, the musician was grinning. "Didn't take you long to stake a claim, did it?" he said. "Mad Max strikes again."

Max ignored the remark and unlocked the door to the shop. "Bring Casey's bike in, will you?"

Zephyr followed with the bike. "Where'd you go riding?" he asked.

"We took the paved trail up to the mountain, then I decided to take off on one of the side trails up by the condos." He wheeled the bike into the back room. "It was a steep trail, all washed out from the snowmelt. Casey took a fall, banged up her knee."

"Guess that route was a little gnarly for a city chick," Zephyr said. "Next time, I'll go with you. Since I've been staying at this dude's house, I know all the trails up there."

"Yeah, we'll ride up there some time." He'd cover more ground with Zephyr along, but it definitely wouldn't be the same.

"That sign you have in the window is wrong, man," Zephyr said as he handed Casey's bike to Max.

"What sign?"

"The one advertising the sale on bike locks. Bicycle is spelled wrong."

Max flushed. "How would you know?"

"Dude!" Zephyr looked offended. "I was an English major." He led the way to the front of the store. "You got the *l* and the *e* reversed."

Max plucked the sign from the display of locks and thrust it at Zephyr. "You fix it, then."

Zephyr shrugged and turned the piece of cardboard over. "Give me a marker and I will."

While Zephyr rewrote the sign, Max studied the other handwritten signs in the store. There weren't very many. Though he was a whiz at math, he tried to avoid showing off his clumsiness when it came to reading and spelling.

Zephyr handed over the corrected sign. "What's wrong with your dog?" he asked.

Max realized Molly had not met them at the door, as she usually did. "What do you mean? What's she doing?"

"She's acting funny. Is she sick or something?"

"What's she doing?" Max asked, emerging from the store room.

"Pacing and whining, panting." Zephyr made a face. "She doesn't look good at all."

Max followed his gaze to the dog, who had flopped down onto the rug in front of the woodstove and was panting heavily. His heart skipped a beat. "You doofus, she's not sick." Max punched Zephyr's shoulder. "She's getting ready to have her puppies." He raced out of the shop and took the steps up to his apartment two at a time. He needed towels, and some old blankets for Molly to lie on. And maybe a big box or basket to help keep the babies corralled.

"What do you want me to do?" Zephyr asked, following him. "Boil water or something?"

"Get Casey," he called over his shoulder. She'd probably be a lot more help in this situation than Zephyr. And she'd definitely be better company.

Chapter Six

"Remind me if I ever have a baby to not let Zephyr anywhere near me when I'm in labor," Casey whispered to Max. The two of them were seated on the floor near the woodstove, with Molly stretched out on a bed of old towels beside them. As the dog panted and whined, Zephyr paced back and forth.

"Are you sure I don't need to boil water or something?" Zephyr asked. "Or, like, time the contractions or measure something? Isn't that what they do on those medical shows?"

Max leaned back on his hands. "This is a dog. They pretty much do all the work. We're just here to keep her company. Didn't you have dogs when you were a kid?"

"Sure." Zephyr stopped and pulled his cap down tighter over his dreadlocks. "We had all kinds of dogs when I was a kid. I love dogs. I'd have a dog now except the musician's life-style isn't really good for a pet. You know, with all the late hours and the traveling and stuff."

Max snorted. "What do you mean, traveling? You never go anywhere."

"Well, not right now, but I could." Zephyr straightened. "You never know when I'm going to be discovered. Then I have to be in a position to drop everything and go, you know?"

Max shook his head and looked at Casey. "What about you? Did you have dogs when you were a kid?"

She shook her head. "My mother thought animals were too much trouble." Her mother also thought children were a lot of trouble, which was probably why Casey was an only child. She stroked Molly's soft head as the dog tensed. "Something's happening," she said.

"Let me see." Zephyr leaned over them.

As they watched, a bloody package slid from Molly. The dog sniffed, then broke the sack and furiously licked at the puppy that emerged. Casey felt a lump in her throat as she watched the mother nuzzle her baby.

"This is so amazing," Zephyr said. "The miracle of birth and everything. I—" He let out a moan and toppled to the floor.

Casey looked around, alarmed, but Max was laughing. "The miracle of birth made him faint," he said. He leaned over and patted his friend on the cheek. "Come on, Zeph. Time to wake up."

Zephyr groaned and rubbed his head, then sat up slowly. "What happened?"

"You fainted," Max said.

Zephyr grimaced. "Guess it's my artistic temperament, you know."

Casey laughed and turned back to Molly. "Here comes another one!" She watched in amazement as yet another little brown puppy was born.

"Uh, I think I'd better get back to the house," Zephyr said. He stood and backed toward the door. "It's almost time to, uh, feed the goldfish." He exited, slamming the door behind him.

"Guess it's a good thing he's a musician instead of a veterinarian," Casey said.

"That's okay," Max said. "He really is a good musician. And a pretty awesome snowboarder, too." He patted Molly. "That's the thing about people in this town. They're all multitalented."

"All of them?" Casey asked. Was that a requirement for living here she'd somehow overlooked?

"Sure. Zephyr plays electric guitar. Hagan can speak Norwegian and ski like a fiend." He ticked the list off on his fingers. "Trish makes the best cup of coffee in town and holds the women's record for the cross-country ski race. Bryan has won the liar's competition at Vinotok three years in a row and Heather once studied to be an opera singer."

"She did?" Casey stared at him. "I don't know whether to be impressed or appalled that you know so much about everyone."

He shrugged. "That's life in a small town. So what's your talent?"

She sat back on her heels. "I don't think I have one." She'd hoped that the move here would teach her her strengths and give her some idea what she was supposed to do with her life. So far, though, nothing had shown up, though she was accumulating a list of things she wasn't good at, including mountain biking, following her mishap this morning.

"You must have a talent," he said. "Heather says you're great with the marketing stuff for the chamber."

"That's a job, not a talent. I mean, I'm competent, but it's not like all the big ad agencies in Chicago were fighting to hire me." Not that she'd *wanted* them to. She enjoyed her work, but her life's ambition was not to be a marketing superstar.

"You can do all kinds of things, I'm sure," Max said.

"Oh, sure, I can do all kinds of things," she said. "None of them very practical. I know how to set the table for a formal dinner. And I know all the proper terms of address for dignitaries from around the world, but unless I run into the Emir of Qatar on the ski slopes, that's not going to be very useful here."

"No kidding? So what do you call an emir?"

"Your highness. An emir is a prince."

He grinned. "My folks would love you. My mom actually reads etiquette books for fun."

An unexpected flutter disturbed her stomach. Did the fact that his parents would approve of her mean that Max didn't? For all the affection in his voice when he spoke of them, he seemed to take a dim view of his parents' conventional life. "She and my mother have something in common, then," she said.

"There must be something you can do that no one else can," Max said. "I'm sure of it."

She thought. "Well, there is one thing, but I don't know if I'd call it a talent."

"What is that?"

Feeling silly, she said, "I can walk on my hands." She'd taught herself one bored summer when she was in the fourth grade. Her friends had been impressed and her parents predictably appalled.

"No kidding?" He looked delighted. "I bet you're a hit at parties."

"There's not much call for that sort of thing at the parties I've attended." Not many people even knew about this particular talent, since her best friend, Mindy Umberger, had moved away in eighth grade.

"I never knew anyone else who could walk on her hands." He stood. "Show me."

"Oh, no," she protested, sorry she'd even brought it up. "I don't want to upset Molly."

"You're not going to upset her. She's fine."

She glanced at the dog. There were four puppies now. Molly was busy licking and nuzzling them. "All right."

She stood and walked to the center of the room, away from furniture and other obstacles. She had discovered last year she could still walk on her hands after a yoga class in which the instructor taught everyone a posture that resembled a handstand. Casey had been the only one in the room to get it on the first try and the only one who was ever able to move around in that position.

"Do you need me to spot you or anything?" Max asked.

"No, I'm good." She rubbed her hands together, then bent and placed them flat on the ground. Carefully shifting her body, she balanced her weight over her shoulders and began moving forward.

"That's awesome," Max cheered.

She smiled and took a few more steps around the room. She had a good view of the underside of tables and chairs. The world definitely looked different turned upside down— it was a new perspective, but tough to navigate. Sort of how she'd felt since coming to Crested Butte.

It was also impossible to look elegant or beautiful while walking on one's hands. The blood rushed to her face, turning it bright red, and there was the problem of her clothing slipping toward her neck and bunching at her knees.

She popped to her feet again, a little out of breath, and smoothed her clothes. "That was great," Max said, and hugged her to him.

The move surprised her. Her arms went around him involuntarily, enjoying his closeness and his strength. He smiled down at her. "You really are amazing," he said. Then he kissed her.

She responded as if she'd been kissing him for years, arching to him and opening her mouth, inviting his tongue.

He made a pleasurable sound and deepened the kiss, his hands sliding down her back to draw her closer still.

So much of the time lately, she felt unsure of herself; Max's arms were one of the few places where everything seemed right.

Only when he broke off the kiss did common sense insist on nudging aside some of her wonder. She looked up at him, a little out of breath and tingling to her toes. "What was that for?" she asked.

"Because I wanted to." His eyes remained locked to hers. "I enjoyed our kiss earlier."

"I did, too," she agreed. But she couldn't help thinking things were happening awfully fast here; experience told her she should be more cautious. "I'm not sure it's smart for me to be kissing you." She took a step back. She'd be able to think clearer standing farther from him.

"Why is that?" he asked.

"Trish told me the first day I was here you were a heart-breaker."

"Are you afraid of having your heart broken because of Paul?"

The mention of Paul startled her. "Paul didn't break my heart," she said. The real problem was Paul had never had her heart in the first place, though it had been almost too late before she realized it.

"You don't have to worry about me," Max said. "I've never deliberately hurt a woman. And we don't have to rush in to anything serious. We can take our time and just get to know each other. Just have fun."

Fun. He made a relationship sound so easy and enjoyable—two things that had been lacking in her relationship with Paul. No strings. No complications. No worries. She nodded. "That sounds good."

He knelt beside Molly once more and felt her abdomen. "Still feels like there might be a couple in there."

"How many is she going to have?" Casey asked, alarmed.

"She's a big dog. She could have ten or twelve or more."

Casey looked at the dog again. "Are you up to it, girl? I'm glad humans don't have to deal with so many babies at once."

"Fortunately, puppies grow up fast."

"Unlike some humans," she quipped, thinking of Zephyr. And to some extent, Max. Not that he was immature, but his emphasis on fun wasn't like most adults she knew.

But she was one to talk. Hadn't her parents reminded her at every opportunity how irresponsible she was to drop everything and move halfway across the country where she knew no one, to a lifestyle completely different from anything she'd ever known?

She knelt beside Max and reached out to stroke one of the warm, wriggly puppies. Maybe Max had the right idea after all—she should focus on enjoying now and not worry so much about the future. Stop worrying about doing the right thing and just do *something*. From that perspective, maybe she and Max were a perfect pair after all.

She watched as two more puppies were born, then Max announced that was probably all. Molly looked exhausted, but happy—not that golden retrievers could ever look unhappy, what with the perpetual smile they wore. She lay back on the blankets and allowed the pups to nurse while she napped. Soon the whole new family was sleeping.

"I'll leave food and water for her to get when she's ready," Max said. He stood and stretched, his shirt pulling up to reveal his flat, muscular abdomen.

Casey looked away, pretending sudden interest in a poster of Moab, Utah, on his wall.

"I'm starved," Max said. "Want to go get something to eat?"

She rose and brushed dog hair from her pants. Was *this* an invitation for a date? "Should I change clothes?"

"Nah, you look fine. We'll go someplace informal."

They ended up at The Last Steep bar and grill, seated in an old wooden booth beneath black-and-white photos of grim-faced skiers from Crested Butte's past. Casey studied the menu. "Everything looks good," she said. "I feel hungry enough to eat it all."

"No need to limit ourselves." He collected the menus and handed them to the waiter who approached. "Give us one of every appetizer, then bring one of every dessert," he said.

Casey laughed. "Appetizer and dessert? Just those?"

"That's the best part of a meal, don't you think? Besides, it'll be like eating at one of those fancy Spanish places."

"Tapas." She nodded. "Or like dim sum at a Chinese place."

"Yeah, like that."

They ordered drinks—margaritas in salt-frosted glasses. The first one tasted so good she knew she drank it too fast, but told herself it didn't matter. She didn't have to drive anywhere or do anything but go back to her place, take a shower and go to bed.

"Have you really met an Emir?" Max asked as he sampled their first course—potato skins, nachos, fried onion strips, bacon-wrapped shrimp and spinach dip with pita chips.

"Yes. My father is assistant to the mayor of Chicago, so we went to a lot of parties with dignitaries."

"Who's your favorite celebrity you've met?" he asked.

She considered the question while she crunched nachos.

"Princess Diana visited the city when I was fifteen," she said after a moment. "I stood in the receiving line to shake her hand and she actually stopped to talk to me for a minute. I think she asked me about school or something." She grinned, remembering.. "I was so awestruck. She was so beautiful."

"I met Matt Damon when he was in town once," Max said. "Except I didn't know who he was until someone told me."

She laughed. "I'll admit most of the celebrities and dignitaries at those parties I attended with my parents didn't impress me," she said. "Mostly, I was bored having to stand around and make conversation with people I hardly knew."

"I'll bet it was a relief when you got older and didn't have to do that anymore," he said.

She stopped in the act of reaching for a potato skin. "Actually, when I got older, I had to attend even *more* boring political functions."

"Why?"

She shifted in her chair. How could she explain this to a man like Max, a man who wouldn't dream of letting someone else tell him what to do? "My parents expected it. My friends expected it, too." It was what young women of her social station did. Never mind if they actually *enjoyed* themselves; making appearances was more valued than enjoyment by the invisible people who dictated such rules.

She shrugged and scooped sour cream onto the potato skin. "It was easier to go along than fight about it."

"Now that you're here, you don't ever have to do that again if you don't want," he said. "Nobody in Crested Butte gives a fig about high society balls. We don't even consider it a good party unless costumes are involved. Preferably goofy costumes."

She laughed. "One of the many things I love about this place."

"What about Paul? I guess he was part of the formal ball crowd?"

She looked away. "Yes." Paul had been right in there with her father, shaking hands, making contacts, nursing his own political aspirations. She'd often felt like no more than a suitable accessory hanging off his arm at such affairs. She didn't care to remember those times. "The appetizers are great," she said, changing the subject. "I hope I have room for dessert."

Somehow she found room for a good helping of fudge cake and a few bites of peach pie. By the time they'd paid the check, she could have rolled out of the restaurant, she was so full. But she walked instead, down the street and up the stairs to their apartments.

At her door, she turned to Max, anticipating a good-night kiss. After all, the two they'd already shared today had been pretty special. Number three was liable to be spectacular.

But instead of pulling her close and kissing her, Max merely patted her shoulder. "I'd better go check on Molly and her pups now. See you tomorrow. Good night."

"Good night," she managed to reply, staring after him. Unlike Paul, who was painfully predictable, Max continually kept her off guard. One minute she was sure they were headed toward a romantic relationship, the next he was treating her like his kid sister.

Maybe the answer was to aim for something in between— friends with benefits? She shook her head. It was early days yet. She'd follow Max's lead and take things slowly, see what developed. They might end up as friends or as lovers, but one thing was for sure, a relationship with Max would be as different from anything she'd known before as a five-course formal dinner was from a meal of only appetizers and desserts.

HEATHER RETURNED FROM VACATION a week later looking well-rested and very tanned. "I had a good time," she told Casey her first morning back at work. "But I'm glad to be home. There's only so much of a fantasy world like that a person can take. Not to mention it's too hot in Florida for my thin blood."

"You look great," Casey said. "But I'm really glad to have you back, too."

"What did you do while I was away?" Heather asked. "Did anything interesting happen?"

"I got a bike. Max and I went for a ride up to Crested Butte Mountain and I fell and scraped up my knee." *And he kissed me.* "Oh, and Molly had her puppies." *And Max kissed me again.* "They're adorable. Four brown ones, a brown-and-white one and a black one."

"Don't tell Emma. When she finds out she'll want one. I've tried to tell her two dogs and a cat are enough, but she's crazy about animals."

"I think most of them are already spoken for." She'd gotten into the habit of stopping by the shop every morning and afternoon to say hello to Molly and check on the pups, who were getting bigger every day. But she couldn't deny her ulterior motive of wanting to see Max. Despite the two kisses they'd shared, the man was unnervingly casual. He greeted her warmly, but with no more heat than he would have greeted Hagan or Trish or even Zephyr. Was he waiting for her to make the next move—or intentionally trying to slow things down between them? It was maddening!

"I was hoping maybe you and Max might get together while everyone was away," Heather said. She gave Casey a questioning look. "Did you?"

It was the perfect opening, so Casey took it. "We went on

the bike ride, and he took care of my knee when I fell. Then he kissed me."

"Oooh, this sounds promising." Heather leaned closer. "And then?"

"And then—not much." She shrugged. "Is he always this way with women—pushing forward, then pulling back? I can't tell if he's waiting for me to make the next move or he wants things to cool off."

Heather considered the question. "Maybe a little of both," she said. "He hasn't had all that many steady relationships since I've known him. He tends to date several different women casually. He has lots of friends, but no one *serious* relationship. Max doesn't do serious very well."

Casey's heart sank. "That's the picture I got from him, too. I don't understand it."

Heather shrugged. "Some men—too many—are afraid of intimacy. Of course, they'd all tell you they're not afraid of anything—they're just being practical."

Casey nodded and went back to sorting through the morning's mail. She liked Max a lot—more than any man she'd met in a long time. She liked his sense of humor and his good looks and the gentle way he treated Molly. And the way he kissed her. But at twenty-six she'd already made so many mistakes in her life she wasn't eager to make another one. Mistakes like getting serious about a man who saw her only as a friend.

"What about you?" Heather asked.

"Hmm?" She looked up, so lost in thought she was sure she must have missed something Heather said. "What did you say?"

Heather scooted her chair closer and lowered her voice to a confidential tone. "Not to be nosy—but I am. What's your relationship history? In particular, who keeps sending you all those letters you shred?"

Casey felt the heat rush to her face. She busied herself sorting through the stack of mail, not seeing any of it. Her whole ill-fated romance with Paul was so embarrassing. "Promise you won't tell a soul?" she asked.

Heather scooted closer still, until her knees were practically touching Casey's. "Not a soul. I promise."

Casey sighed. Maybe it would be good for her to tell someone. "Paul was my fiancé."

"No!" Heather's eyes widened. "Is that why you're here? Because he broke your heart? And now he's trying to get you back and you won't have anything to do with him?"

Casey looked at her friend a long moment. It would be so easy to let Heather think she'd hit on the truth. Easy and much more flattering to Casey herself. But she wasn't comfortable with the lie. "More like I broke his heart," she said. "I realized I was only marrying him because my parents liked him so much and because we'd been dating so long everyone expected it."

"So you realized you didn't love him and broke up with him." Heather leaned over and covered Casey's hand with her own. "That took a lot of guts. Did it cause a lot of trouble with your family?"

She nodded. "Oh, yes." Her stomach still ached when she thought about that awful day.

"How long had you been engaged?" Heather asked.

"A year." She winced, waiting for Heather to object. Everyone else she knew certainly had. "I wasn't trying to lead him on, honestly," she said. "I just got so caught up in all the hype and the wedding preparations and everything. And you might not believe it now, but most of my life I've done exactly what was expected of me." She'd tried a few minor rebellions when she was younger—lobbying to attend public school at one point, adopting an outrageous hairstyle at another—but her parents had gotten very good at ignoring such outbursts and bringing her back into line.

She sneaked a glance at Heather and was relieved to see her friend still looked sympathetic. "I'm sure you're not the only woman who's been caught up in a similar situation," Heather said. "At least you had the sense to break things off before the wedding."

"Well…" She rubbed her thumb along the edge of the desk, searching for the right words. "I didn't exactly break it off *before* the wedding."

"You didn't marry him, did you?" Heather's eyes widened. "What? Did you, like, have the marriage annulled or something?"

Casey shook her head. "No, we never went through with our vows."

She could tell the instant Heather realized the truth. Her eyes got even wider and her mouth dropped open. "You decided *at* the wedding?" she said. "Were you standing at the altar and decided you couldn't go through with it?"

"Not at the altar," Casey said. "I was in the bride's room before the ceremony." Her mother had just finished pinning her veil in place and they'd stood together, admiring her reflection in the full-length mirror on one wall. Casey had considered the stranger who stared back at her and recognized the panic in her own eyes. "I knew if I went out there and said my vows, I'd be trapped in a life I didn't want," she said. "I didn't want to be Mrs. Paul Rittinghouse. I didn't want to chair the Junior League and support all the right charities and be a lovely accessory to my husband's political career. I realized I was twenty-six years old and I'd never done one thing I really wanted to do."

Heather sat back, hands in her lap. "So you called off the wedding?"

She nodded. "I told my mother I wasn't going through with it and I gave my engagement ring to my maid of honor and told her to give it to Paul. Then I locked myself in the bathroom. By the time my parents got a locksmith to open the door, I'd changed out of my wedding dress, crawled out a window and flagged down a taxi. I hid in a hotel for two days until things had calmed down a little." She'd spent most of those two days crying and drinking every little bottle from the hotel minibar, even the weird liquors she didn't really like.

"You were a runaway bride!" Heather laughed. "That's amazing. Were your parents really upset?"

Casey nodded. "Oh, yes. At one point, my mother threatened to have me committed, but my father managed to calm her down. He wasn't crazy about the way I'd embarrassed the family—those were his exact words, I had 'let everyone down and embarrassed the family'—and he wasn't excited about having laid out all that money for a wedding that never happened. But he knew I wasn't crazy." She sighed. "I spent the next two weeks returning gifts and writing letters of apology to all the guests. I apologized to Paul, too."

"How did he take it?"

She frowned. "In some ways, not as badly as I would have expected from someone who was supposed to be in love with me. He seemed more focused on the embarrassment angle, too. And he sided with my mother on the question of my sanity. He apparently couldn't believe any woman in her right mind *wouldn't* want to marry him." She smiled slightly at the memory. "If he'd fallen on his knees and pledged his undying love, I would have felt guiltier about leaving him in the lurch. As it was, every time I talked to him he confirmed the rightness of my decision."

"But he still writes to you," Heather said. "So he must feel something."

She nodded. "As long as I've known him—and he's been a friend of my family's for years—Paul has had his whole life planned out, to the last detail. When he was nine, he knew that he would one day attend Princeton and receive a degree in political science, then attend Harvard Law School like his father. Then he would take a job at his father's firm and from there would move into politics. At age thirty, he would marry. He told me when I was sixteen that he had decided two years earlier that I would be his wife, because I met all his requirements for the perfect mate. I was the right age, came from a suitable family and since my father was a diplomat, I already possessed all the skills to serve as a political hostess."

"My God, he makes you sound like an applicant for a secretarial position or something."

"Or something."

"I'd say you did the right thing getting out of that situation," Heather said. "And you did right coming to Crested Butte, too. No one here is going to expect you to act 'suitably' or do anything at all you don't want to do."

She nodded. "I knew if I stayed in Chicago they'd eventually wear me down. They always have before. So moving seemed the only course."

"Does Max know any of this?" Heather asked.

"No!" She turned to her friend, alarmed. "And don't you dare tell him. I don't want anyone to know."

"I won't tell him. I promise. But now that I know the truth, I think Max is perfect for you. You couldn't find someone less like Paul. Max doesn't care what anyone thinks and I doubt his plans extend into next week, much less the rest of his life." She sat back in her chair and looked thoughtful. "Of course, that's the problem with a lot of men in this town—they *think* they're not ready for commitment, when actually that's exactly what they need. They just need the right woman to show them the truth."

Something in Heather's voice made Casey wary. "I don't know… I don't think you can set out to try to change someone," she said. "Especially a man."

"You don't let them *know* what you're up to, of course," she said. "But there are some men around here—Max is one of them—who could stand to have their eyes opened."

"You aren't thinking of a certain hunky Norwegian, are you?" Casey asked.

Heather's cheeks turned pink. "Hagan is thirty-four years old. I can't believe his playboy bachelor routine isn't getting a little old."

Casey shook her head. "I don't know, Heather. I don't think Hagan—or Max—is going to change just because you want him to. And we could end up looking like fools if we try."

Heather gave her a challenging look. "And I say a determined women is no match for any man. I'm tired of spending my vacations—and my nights—alone. And I'm going to find some way to make Hagan see he's the perfect man for me."

The ringing telephone cut short their conversation, but Casey pondered Heather's words all morning. Was Max the perfect man for *her?* And if so, to what lengths should she go to get him and *keep* him?

She couldn't go along with Heather's plan to chase after a man. She might end up with the man of her dreams, but then again, she might just be chasing after trouble.

Chapter Seven

"The trouble with women is that they mess with your head too much." Max offered this opinion to Hagan as the two of them clung to the side of a rock face, slowly making their way to the cliff above.

Hagan grunted in what Max took to be agreement and pulled himself up another few feet, his fingers digging into a small crevice and his toes balancing on slight irregularities in the rock. "It's not that they mess with your head so much," Hagan said after a moment. "It's that when you are with a pretty one, most of your blood rushes south so you can't think straight."

Max could admit there was some truth to Hagan's theory, at least where Casey was concerned. The powerful physical attraction he felt for her might be partly to blame for the confusion he experienced whenever he was with her. The two kisses they'd shared had been mind-blowing—definitely in the top five kisses of all time. Which is one reason he'd put the brakes on since then. He wasn't sure he really wanted his mind blown.

Clinging tightly to the rock with one hand, he stretched the other arm overhead and felt blindly for a handhold. He found a crevice and wedged his chalked fingers into it, then heaved himself up, muscles straining. "Casey and I went biking while everyone was out of town," he said.

"Huh." Hagan dragged himself up farther, sending a shower of gravel cascading down. "So she's the woman messing with your head now."

"Yeah." Max tested a foothold to see if it would bear his weight, then stepped up. "I really like her. She's fun to be with. Smart. Good sense of humor."

"Then what is the problem?" Hagan looked up to gauge the distance to the top of the cliff and climbed another few inches.

"She's almost *too* perfect." Max grunted and scrambled up until he reached the top, then hauled himself over and turned to help Hagan.

The two men lay panting for a moment, looking down the slope they'd just ascended. The steep rock face loomed over a deep, rocky canyon where aspen and scrub oak were thick and green.

After a moment, Hagan rolled onto his back and stretched his arms over his head. "There's no such thing as a perfect woman," he said. "Much less *too perfect.*"

"My parents would think Casey was perfect," Max said. He rolled onto his back also, and shaded his eyes with one hand. "She's educated, cultured. She didn't say, but I'm betting she comes from money. I can't figure out what she's doing out here. None of the usual things that apply to women who end up here apply to her. She doesn't ski or snowboard and she'd apparently never been on a mountain bike before the day I took her out. She didn't follow some guy out here. She doesn't have relatives here."

"She doesn't sound perfect at all, then. At least not for you.

Haven't you always said you wanted a real outdoors woman? Someone who enjoyed the same things you enjoyed. So what are you worried about?"

He was worried because, despite the fact that Casey didn't fit the image he had of the perfect woman for him, when he was with her everything felt so *right.* "I didn't say she didn't enjoy the same things I enjoy. We had a great time on our bike ride. Casey's game for anything. But some things about her make me nervous."

Hagan laughed. "You, nervous? She *is* messing with your head. I told you, no good comes of getting involved with local women. If you do as I do and date women who are only in town for a few days, there's no problem with either of you mistaking what you have for anything permanent."

"She's got some guy from Chicago—Paul somebody— who writes to her all the time. At least once a week."

"Old boyfriend?" Hagan asked.

"Something like that. She never reads the letters, she just shreds them. I wonder what that's all about."

"Have you asked her?"

Max frowned. "I got the impression she didn't want to talk about it."

"You'll never know if you don't ask."

He glared at his friend. "I don't know why I'm talking to you about this. You're not exactly an expert when it comes to women."

"I know how to enjoy them without getting all tied in a knot over it," Hagan said. He smiled. "For instance, I had a very enjoyable time with a certain shapely brunette on my fishing trip to Canada. Bertrice was the sister of a fishing guide there and she offered to show me some of her favorite spots."

"Did you catch a lot of fish?"

Hagan laughed. "Whoever said Bertrice and I went fishing?"

Max sat up and studied his friend. Nothing ever seemed to shake Hagan, but sometimes Max suspected his carefree demeanor hid deeper emotions. "Don't you ever want more from a relationship with a woman than sex?" he asked. "Aren't you ever tempted to stick around and get to know some of these women better? To let them know you?"

Hagan sat also, and busied himself tying the lace of one climbing shoe. "Tempted? Yes, I have been tempted." He stood. "But then I remind myself that it is always better to be the one leaving than the one left." He began gathering his climbing gear. "Let's head back into town," he said. "You got me out of bed too early this morning. I need some caffeine."

Max stood and began coiling rope and unclipping carabiners. He wondered who—or more specifically, what *woman*—in Hagan's past had given him such an aversion to being left, but he knew better than to ask. Guys didn't talk about such things, though maybe some night, over a few beers, he'd find out more.

"COFFEE. After a day like today, I need serious caffeine." Heather locked the chamber of commerce office and pocketed the key.

"Sounds good to me," Casey said. She and Heather had finalized arrangements for the upcoming Bike Fest, including arranging accommodations for the sponsors' reps, finalizing the race route, making sure the proper permits were in order and arranging for cleanup. It was enough to wear out anybody.

The two women crossed the street and headed down Elk Avenue toward the coffee shop. The weather was warm enough now for shirtsleeves and it seemed to Casey that the town had transformed almost overnight from winter to summer. Instead of the snowdrifts that had greeted her when she arrived in town, flower boxes and barrels decorated storefronts. Boutiques advertised shorts and sandals instead of sweaters and boots, and bicycles had replaced snowboards in Mad Max's display window. Half the cars that cruised by were equipped with bicycle racks and water bowls had been set up outside several shops to quench the thirst of passing dogs.

Trish waved at them from behind the counter when they entered, then turned to wait on a quartet of tourists lined up in front of them. Even Casey could easily identify the visitors by the multiple shopping bags draped over their arms.

"What'll it be, ladies?" Trish asked when it was Heather and Casey's turn. "Special of the day is a Sumatra dark roast. Great with a shot of chocolate."

"I recommend it," Zephyr called from a stool at the end of the counter. He held up his cup. "Extra good with a shot of caramel."

"Sounds good to me." Heather dropped into a chair at a small table near the door. "How's business?"

"Good." Trish added two squirts of chocolate syrup to a paper cup and topped it off with coffee. "Same for you?" she asked Casey.

"Thanks. It sounds good." Casey took out her purse. "I'll buy today," she said, waving Heather back into her chair. "You can get it next time."

"Of course it's good." Trish assumed an expression of mock outrage. "The reason we don't have a Starbucks here is because they know they couldn't compete with me."

"That, and the local abhorrence of chain stores," Heather said. She accepted a steaming cup from Casey, who joined her at the table. "It's one of the things that makes Crested Butte unique."

"Speaking of unique—" Zephyr got up and joined them at the table "—do either of you ladies know of a place my band could use to practice?"

"What's wrong with wherever you practice now?" Heather asked.

Zephyr adopted a hangdog look. "We've been practicing at the drummer's house, but he's moving to a new place and his landlady says no way does she want us over there."

"Who's his new landlady?" Heather asked.

Zephyr's face grew even longer. "That would be his girlfriend, Stasia. He's moving in with her and she doesn't much like us."

"I can't imagine why," Heather said, winking at Casey, who turned away to hide a smile. Not that Zephyr wasn't a great guy, but as far as she could tell, his band played all types of music, as long as they were loud.

The door opened and the small shop was suddenly full of men. Actually only two men—Max and Hagan—but their presence filled the space. Dressed in cargo shorts and T-shirts, exposing expanses of bronzed muscle and glowing with a slight sheen of sweat, they drew the eye of everyone in the room.

"What have you two been up to?" Trish asked as she wiped down the front counter.

"We spent the day climbing in Taylor canyon," Max said. He leaned on one hand against the counter and studied the menu board. "Give me an extra-large mocha on ice," he said.

"Large espresso," Hagan said. He folded his arms across his chest; Casey thought she heard Heather sigh.

Trish turned to the espresso machine and began measuring ground coffee. "All right, but I might have to ask you two to take these outside," she said. "All this testosterone is wilting my flowers."

"I can wilt flowers," Zephyr protested.

"Your breath, maybe," Trish said cheerfully.

"Hey Zephyr, ladies." Max nodded to them. "What's up?" He nudged Casey's shoulder. "How was your day?"

"Good." She smiled, amazed at how a simple question and a casual touch could make her feel so good—and more than a little breathless.

"I was just telling Heather and Casey how my band is looking for a new place to rehearse," Zephyr said. "Do you know of anybody who would let us use their space?"

Max shook his head. "Not offhand, but if I hear of anything, I'll let you know."

"While you're at it, if you hear of any jobs, let me know about that, too," Zephyr said. "The people I'm house-sitting for are moving back to town for the summer, so I need to find another source of income. At least until this music thing really takes off."

Max managed to keep a straight face, though Hagan coughed and looked away. "I might be able to help you out with the job thing," Max said. "Rob, the guy who works for me part-time, is moving back to Fort Collins in another week. You know about bikes and snowboards, right?"

"Dude! I'm all about bikes and snowboards. And guitars."

"No guitars, but I could use someone who knows his way around a bike. It's only twenty-four hours a week."

"That's cool. I have to leave time for the band." Zephyr's face brightened. "Say, do you think after hours the guys and I could—"

"No."

Zephyr started to stand. "But if you're closed—"

"Casey and I live upstairs, remember." Max clapped him on the shoulder. "You can start work in a week. Stop by sometime before then to fill out the paperwork."

Zephyr sat again. "Thanks. And let me know if you hear of anybody with a place where we can rehearse. A barn or a porch or anything. Somebody who's willing to support the arts, you know?"

"They've been having trouble with bears getting into the Dumpsters over by the Irwin Campground," Hagan said. He came to stand beside their table. "Maybe your band could practice out there and scare them off."

"You think so?" Zephyr grinned. "Maybe the forest service would even pay us. Call it bear mitigation or something."

"Aren't there noise ordinances in those campgrounds?" Max handed Hagan his coffee. "Don't listen to him, Zeph. He's just trying to cause trouble."

Hagan gave a wicked grin, but said nothing.

"We'd better go before Trish runs us out," Max said. He raised his cup in a salute. "See you all later." His words were for everyone, but Casey was sure he was looking only at her when he said them.

"Yeah, see you," she said softly. She couldn't have stopped smiling if she wanted to.

As the bells on the door jangled in their wake, Heather made a show of fanning herself.

"What's the matter, Heather?" Zephyr asked. "Is it too warm in here?"

"Oh, it's hot in here, all right," she said. Her eyes looked feverish, her expression verging on desperate.

Casey ducked her head. She could sympathize with her friend. She was all but panting over Max herself. There was something about a man who was so overtly, well, *masculine*. It was enough to make any woman forget herself. But she reminded herself she needed to be careful. She didn't want to make a fool of herself in front of a lot of people. She'd done that once already, when she'd called off her wedding. There was probably a limit to how many times a person could do that sort of thing and still have an ego left.

LATER THAT AFTERNOON, Max stopped Casey on her way in to her apartment. His hair was damp and she could smell the herbal shampoo he used. A disconcerting fantasy of him in the shower flashed through her mind and she struggled to stay composed.

"Come in a minute and see the puppies," he said. "Their eyes are open now."

She followed him into his living room, where she was greeted by Molly, puppies tumbling along behind her. Casey dropped to her knees on the rug and they happily engulfed her. They were wriggling bundles of fur and pink tongues, gazing up at her with liquid brown eyes. "They're adorable," she exclaimed. She picked up the lone black pup and snuggled it against her cheek. She couldn't remember ever feeling anything so soft.

"They're crawling all over the place now," Max said, sitting beside her on the rug. "When I'm gone I have to barricade them in the kitchen. Molly can hop over the gate and go out to get a break from them, though they all press up against the gate and whine until she returns."

She turned the pup she held to face her. "You miss your mommy, don't you?" she said, only slightly self-conscious about speaking in baby talk before Max. But puppies seemed to demand such behavior. She placed the black pup among its siblings and chose one of the golden ones to cuddle next.

"Which one do you want for yours?" Max asked.

She almost dropped the puppy, she was so startled. She stared at him. "What do you mean?"

He grinned. "If you're going to live here, you need a dog."

He nodded to the puppies. "I thought I'd give you first choice."

She set the puppy gently on the rug and studied the writhing, tumbling mass of little bodies. "I've never had a pet before," she said.

"You told me that, but it's not like owning a dog is rocket science. And I'll be right here to answer any questions you have."

"Aren't they a little young to leave their mother?" she asked, stalling, giving herself time to absorb the idea of being responsible for another creature.

"Of course. They need to stay with her until they're weaned. Another six weeks or so. But people are already stopping by, wanting to lay claim to one." He shifted and pointed to the black pup. "That and that brown one with the curly tail are girls. All the rest are males."

The black pup crawled over and began to lick her hand. It felt like being caressed by warm satin. "I think I'd like this one," she said, picking up the pup and cradling it in her hand. "If you're sure."

"I'm sure." He grinned. The way his eyes lit up when he smiled sent a tremor through her middle. Max wasn't the most talkative guy in the world, but he sure said a lot with his eyes.

The puppy she held yipped, distracting her from her silent conversation with Max. "What should I name her?" she asked.

"I don't know." He stroked the pup with one finger. "When I name dogs, I usually try out a few I like until I find one that seems to fit the animal."

She studied the puppy, who was now sprawled across her knee on its stomach. "I think I'll call her Lucy," she said. She didn't know why—the name had just popped into her head. She glanced at him. "She looks like a Lucy, don't you think?"

He laughed. "If you say so."

Molly had laid down and Lucy's brothers and sister swarmed over their mother, fighting for a place to nurse. Casey settled Lucy in next to her siblings. Now that she'd claimed the pup as hers, she hated to let it go. She'd be counting the days until Lucy could come and live with her.

She looked at Max again. He was watching her, his gaze like a caress. "Thank you," she said. "I think this might be one of the nicest gifts anyone has ever given me." Her parents had always given her gifts *they* wanted her to have: a rabbit coat when all the girls in her school wore them, expensive electronics a magazine had declared the must-have gift for the season, subscriptions to the right magazines or tickets to the opera or the theater designed to improve her cultural IQ. Paul had given her a diamond ring and other jewelry, but always as a way of showing off how much he could afford to spend on her. This puppy had cost Max nothing, yet it was something so personal— something she could love that would love her in return.

"You're welcome." He leaned toward her, his mouth close to hers. "I have a vested interest in wanting you to have every reason to stay in town," he said.

"Y-you do?" Most of the time, Max acted more like a casual friend than a romantic interest. Other than when he was kissing her, she might have been just another woman. Maybe the gift of Lucy was more than a gift. Maybe it was a silent signal he was ready to take things to the next level.

"I do. I really like you, Casey. I like you a lot." He emphasized this statement with a kiss.

Casey leaned into him, letting the warmth from his lips flow through her all the way down to her toes. It wasn't exactly a declaration of undying love, but then, she wasn't ready for anything so dire. Not yet.

She was trying hard to discover what *she* really wanted. All she had to go on was her gut feeling about whether or not something felt right. Following her gut had led to some interesting choices, from painting her bedroom walls lavender to giving most of her high heels to the local thrift store and buying a new pair of hiking boots. Knowing Max liked her *a lot* and that she felt the same way about him, felt very right indeed.

WARM WEATHER BROUGHT CROWDS of tourists to town. They filled the restaurants and stores and provided a steady stream of traffic to the chamber of commerce offices. A part-time helper, Margie, joined Heather and Casey behind the front counter and they took turns fielding inquiries from visitors. Along with the usual requests for directions, restaurant recommendations and help finding lodging, were more unusual questions. "Where do you keep the elk?" a tall sunburned woman asked one morning in late June. "I want to photograph them."

"Why don't you build steps and railings on the hiking trails?" a man in a madras plaid shirt complained another day. "They're much too steep and not safe at all."

"Why doesn't this town have a movie theater?" another woman asked. "There's nothing to do here." This after Casey had listed no less than ten different activities, including two concerts, a play, several guided hikes, a fly-fishing seminar, a frisbee golf tournament and a community picnic.

"The summer tourists are worse than the winter tourists," Hagan declared one afternoon when he stopped by the chamber offices to deliver a fresh supply of Forest Service campground guides. From Memorial Day to Labor Day, Hagan worked as a seasonal ranger, doing everything from collecting campground fees and cleaning outhouses to leading guided hikes. The summer sun had bleached his hair almost white and a deep tan made his blue eyes stand out even more. Casey had to admit he was an arresting sight in his uniform, a green shirt and shorts and a pair of leather boots. Every woman within view of the chamber offices would suddenly find a reason to stop by when Hagan was there and Heather dropped all pretense of working whenever he showed up.

"Where does the Forest Service have you working these days?" Heather asked, offering him an openly flirtatious smile.

He glanced at her, then back at the brochures he was sorting. "I'm over near Lake Irwin this week, doing trail and campground maintenance."

"Sounds like hard work." She leaned toward him, her chin propped on one hand. "But I know you enjoy being out of doors."

"Hmm." He handed two stacks of brochures to Casey. "There's some campground guides and some trail guides for you."

"Thanks, Hagan."

"You're welcome. I'll see you later." He nodded to Casey and waved vaguely in Heather's direction, then left, most of the women who had just happened to stop by following in his wake.

Heather sat back in her chair. "I think I've finally come up with a way to get his attention," she said.

Casey stifled a groan. She really liked Heather and hated to see her friend set herself up for a heartache. She swivelled her chair around to face Heather. It was Margie's afternoon off and Hagan's exit had left them alone, at least briefly. "Why are you so interested in Hagan when he hasn't done anything to encourage you?" she asked.

Heather shook her head, her blond hair swinging. "That's

where you're wrong. Anybody could have dropped off those brochures this afternoon," she said. "But Hagan chose to do it himself. We know it's not because he's interested in you—he knows you're dating Max and Max is his best friend. So he must have stopped by because he wanted to see me."

"Maybe Hagan's boss told him to deliver the brochures," Casey said.

"No, you just have to know how to read these strong, silent types."

"Heather, the man hardly even talks to you. He scarcely even *looks* at you."

"Exactly! If he wasn't interested, he'd treat me like everyone else. Instead, he's so obviously avoiding me that has to mean he's interested." Her smile was triumphant.

Or maybe Hagan was so aware of Heather's crush on him that he went out of his way to avoid anything that might encourage her, Casey thought. But Heather wasn't in the mood to hear anything that approached logic on the subject of the hunky Norwegian. She sighed. "So what is your plan?" If it was anything too embarrassing, maybe she could talk her friend out of it.

"Hagan volunteers with Search and Rescue, right?"

Casey nodded. "So does Max. So does Bryan and a lot of guys in town."

"Right, but Hagan's also a Forest Ranger, so he has to participate in one capacity or another whenever a hiker is lost or injured on Forest Service lands."

"He does?" Casey was foggy on protocol in these situations.

"He does. So if I'm out hiking and *just happen* to twist my ankle—especially on a day when I know he's working nearby—he'll have to come and rescue me."

"That's ridiculous," Casey protested. "Number one, why

would you purposely injure yourself? And number two, it sound like a bad *I Love Lucy* script."

Heather laughed. "I always loved that show. And I'm not really going to hurt myself. I'll just pretend."

"And you'll look like a fool when Hagan finds out your injury isn't real."

"Oh, I'll fake it well enough. A good fall, a few bruises…" She shrugged. "It will be worth it to make him admit his real attraction."

"*If* he's attracted." Casey scooted her chair over to Heather's desk. "You're a very attractive woman. You have a lot going for you. I hate to see you throw yourself at a man who doesn't appreciate you."

Heather's expression sobered and she nodded. "I know I'm taking a chance. Maybe I *will* come off looking like a fool. But I'm tired of sitting back and waiting for a man to make the first move. At least this way I'll know for sure how Hagan feels. I won't have to guess anymore."

"But you could be really hurt," Casey said.

"I won't be," Heather said. "I've hiked all over these mountains for years and I've never come close to being injured. The only thing that might end up hurt is my pride and I can deal with that."

Casey nodded. She admired Heather's determination and she could relate to a woman doing something others considered foolhardy for the sake of her own peace of mind. "When are you going to do it?" she asked.

"You heard him say he's over by Lake Irwin this week. There are all kinds of trails there. I thought I'd take off Wednesday afternoon and head over there."

"You can't go by yourself," Casey said. She'd handed out enough hiking guides this summer to have memorized the safety rules printed on the front. Number one was *Don't Go Alone.*

Heather gave her a sly smile. "We won't be very busy then. Margie can handle things by herself. If I give you the afternoon off, will you come with me?"

Casey wanted no part of Heather's scheming, but she couldn't let her friend do this on her own.

"You know Max is likely to show up with Hagan," Heather pressed. "Now that he has Zephyr working for him, he's always one of the first responders."

"I can see Max anytime," Casey said. The two of them ate dinner together about half the time now and she'd been on several bike rides with him lately and out for drinks a few times. It was fairly low-key as relationships went—other than a few kisses, nothing physical had happened. His reluctance to take things further was both refreshing and frustrating, but she told herself she was lucky not to have the complication of a relationship in her life right now.

"There's nothing sexier than a hot guy coming to the rescue of a damsel in distress," Heather said. "If Max thought you were in danger, it might snap him out of his let's-just-be-friends nonsense."

Casey shifted in her chair. "Max and I are taking things slowly," she said. "There's nothing wrong with that." After her mistake with Paul, she was in no hurry to rush into anything. So maybe Max seemed a little *overly* cautious, but as well as the two of them got along she had faith their relationship would soon advance to the next level. There was nothing wrong with taking the time to get things right.

"Not for you, maybe." Heather sat back and folded her arms across her chest. "But I'm tired of waiting around. This time, I'm going to *make* something happen. Are you with me or not?"

Casey nodded. "I'm with you." She couldn't allow Heather to do this on her own, even though Casey stood to come off as big a fool as her friend. But so long as she didn't injure anything other than her dignity, she knew she could survive. She'd had plenty of practice lately.

Chapter Eight

Casey hoped Heather would return to her normally sensible self before she actually went through with her scheme to snag Hagan. In the meantime, Casey intended to be there to keep her friend from getting seriously hurt, at least physically. And she couldn't complain about having the afternoon off to go hiking.

"This is partly your fault," Heather said Wednesday afternoon as they set out up a narrow, rocky trail not far from the Lake Irwin campground.

"My fault?" Casey adjusted a strap on her backpack. "How is this my fault?"

"You inspired me, with your story of calling off your wedding at the last minute. That took guts. And look how it's paid off for you."

"How has it paid off?" Casey asked, wary.

"You're living here in this great place, starting life over completely on your own and dating a great guy."

"Well, sort of dating," she said. "Not that I'm complaining, but he certainly doesn't behave like any other man I've dated."

"Did Paul rush you?" Heather stepped over a large rock in the trail.

Casey made a face. "Not exactly. I mean, we dated for two years before he proposed, but almost from the first time we went out he *assumed* that we would always be together. And so did everyone else." She picked her way up a steep section of the trail littered with boulders. "I kept telling myself that this was how love worked—that you were friends with someone and that friendship eventually morphed into love, and even passion. But that never happened with Paul."

"Yet you agreed to marry him."

She nodded. "Everyone said we were so perfect for each other. My mother kept telling me how lucky I was to have a man who was so well-off and who had such a prosperous future ahead. That I'd be a fool to let him get away."

"It sounds like something out of a Jane Austen novel," Heather said. She led the way around a series of switchbacks.

"I guess that's why her books are still popular—they're more contemporary than some people think." Casey stopped a moment to catch her breath. "Anyway, I suppose I ought to be glad Max isn't making any kind of assumptions."

"Today will be good for you." Heather turned to face Casey. "He'll probably show up with Hagan and the possibility that you might have needed rescuing, as well, might be the thing he needs to make him realize how stupid he'd be to let you get away."

Casey shook her head. "I honestly don't think Max is interested in catching anyone—or in being caught. And it's probably a good idea for me not to rush into anything, either. I don't want to make another mistake."

"I'm sure you're right. But I've been cautious long enough. I'm probably overdue for a little recklessness." She started up the trail again. "After Emma's father and I divorced, I was too busy raising Emma and trying to keep my head above water financially to think about dating or the future. Then one day

I looked at a calendar and realized I was past my thirtieth birthday and the prospect of spending the rest of my life alone loomed pretty large."

"Being single isn't exactly a fate worse than death," Casey protested.

"No, but if another option presents itself, I intend to take it." Heather grinned. "And if that option has blond hair, blue eyes and a sexy Norwegian accent…" She stopped halfway up yet another steep section of trail and slipped off her pack. "This looks like a good spot," she said.

Casey stopped beside her and looked around. "Wow." One side of the trail dropped off sharply, opening on a view of the mountains and valley below. Scant patches of snow atop the distant peaks shimmered in the brightness against an impossibly blue sky. "I hope I never stop being awed by the scenery around here," she said.

"Let's hope Hagan is more interested in me than the view," Heather said. She sat on a boulder and contemplated the ground around her. "What we need is a big rock."

"There are big rocks everywhere around here," Casey said. "What do you want one for?"

"I thought you could drop one on my ankle. I don't want to really hurt myself, but I at least need a bruise to be convincing. And a little swelling might be good."

Casey took a step back. "I am *not* going to drop rocks on you!"

Heather frowned. "Maybe you could push me. I probably wouldn't be hurt too badly, but I'd be banged up in the fall." She nodded. "That would probably be more convincing than a few dropped rocks."

"No!" Casey took another step back. "I won't do it. This whole thing is nuts. We should just go home."

Heather appeared on the verge of arguing before she finally slumped. "You're right," she said. "I was crazy to even think it."

Casey was relieved. "I'll help you think of something else later," she said. "Something that isn't so risky."

"We might as well head back." Heather shoved herself off of the boulder, but at the same moment, Casey started to turn around, only to discover she'd backed up to the very edge of the drop-off alongside the trail. She gave a panicked cry and tried to scramble back, but her foot slipped in the loose rock and she went tumbling over the edge.

For a fraction of a second, the thought flashed through Casey's head that she was about to die, followed by the depressing thought that when people spoke of her death in the future, their first words would likely be some comment on her clumsiness.

About this time, she woke up to the fact that the drop-off was not as steep as it had first looked and that, instead of hurtling through space like a character in some cartoon, she was in fact sliding on her stomach down a rocky slope pocked with scrubby trees. She reached out a hand and grasped one of the trees and held on tightly, arresting her slide.

"Casey!" Heather's panicked voice drifted down from overhead. "Casey, are you all right?"

Good question. She did a quick assessment. She was hanging off the side of a mountain, rocks digging into her stomach and thighs, twigs caught in her hair. Her shirt was torn and she was pretty sure the sticky sensation on one leg was blood, though not a great deal of it. She tried to pull herself up to a more secure position and blinding pain shot through her left shoulder. She sagged back, groaning, breathing hard and waiting for the woozy feeling to subside. She refused to pass out. Doing so might mean letting go of the branch and sliding farther down the slope.

"Are you all right?" Heather called down again.

"I've hurt my shoulder!" she shouted up, her voice surprisingly weak. She tried again. "Get help!"

"I'm going to call for help!" Heather responded.

Casey prayed Heather's cell phone actually worked up here. Heather had promised it would, but Casey had already learned how unpredictable communications were in these mountains.

A moment later Heather called to her again. "Search and Rescue is on the way. Oh, Casey, I'm so sorry."

"It's not your fault I'm clumsy," Casey said, but she doubted Heather heard her. And she didn't want to waste her strength shouting anymore. Her shoulder was hurting worse and her right hand and arm were protesting about the strain of holding on to the bush.

She managed to push herself up to a more comfortable position and was able to let go of the bush. She rolled over onto her right side and had an ant's-eye view of rocks and patches of stubby grass and trees. At least it was summer and she wasn't cold.

The thought immediately made her aware of how chilly the ground really was. *Think warm thoughts,* she told herself. She closed her eyes and tried to summon images of sunlit beaches and sweltering days.

Instead, the lacy image of her wedding dress floated in front of her and hot tears stung her eyes. She could have died just now, without ever getting to walk down the aisle in that beautiful dress. More tears overflowed. She hadn't even *thought* of the dress in weeks and suddenly it seemed the most important thing in the world. She *did* want to wear that dress again, and to have the home and family and everything it represented.

Her thoughts drifted, her addled brain replaying snippets

of arguments with her mother, family vacations to the beach, her favorite coffee shop on Michigan Avenue and Max's smiling face, asking if she was all right.

The last was not, in fact, a dream, but the man himself. He half climbed, half slid down beside her, a safety line around his waist providing traction for him to brace against. "Casey, are you all right?" he asked again, his face close to hers.

He was very pale beneath his tan. She smiled up at him. Of all the people she wanted to see right now, he was at the top of her list. Her good friend, Max, who might be so much more. "I'm all right. Except I did something to my shoulder."

"I'm going to fasten this line to you," he said. "Try not to move too much."

She did as he asked, waiting while he clipped her into a safety harness. Knowing she was attached to the line made her feel much more secure and she pushed herself into a sitting position.

"I told you not to move," Max said, not harshly.

"I'm fine, really," she said. "Except for my shoulder." The slightest movement of her left side sent pain shooting through her.

Max felt gingerly along her shoulder and the top of her arm. "It could be dislocated. What happened?"

She flushed. "I got too close to the edge and took a wrong step." It was the truth, though not the whole truth.

"You're just accident-prone when it comes to these mountains, aren't you?" he teased.

"I guess so. And you're always there to pick me up afterward." That seemed significant now. If she needed looking after—and didn't everyone need that at some time or other—then Max was the one to do it. Now and quite possibly... forever?

He examined her leg, which had stopped bleeding. It was the opposite leg from the one she'd hurt bike riding. That knee still bore a scar. "Just a nasty scrape there," he said. "It'll need cleaning up, but it can wait until you're back up top." He opened his pack and took out a blue canvas sling. "I'm going to immobilize your arm with this."

She studied him while he put the sling around her and adjusted it. He was so gentle. A much better fit for her than Paul had been. "Thanks for coming to my rescue again," she said. "It's nice to know I can always count on you."

He looked up from his work. "Hey, what are friends for?" he said, grinning.

"You're more than a friend to me," she said, her expression serious.

His smile weakened. "Uh, yeah." He stood, still holding the hand on her uninjured side. "Stand and I'll help you climb back up. Hagan will be pulling from the top, so it shouldn't be too bad."

"Hagan is here?" At least that part of Heather's plan had come true. She hoped her friend was taking full advantage of the opportunity to be alone with her dream man.

"He was right over at Irwin Lake, so he didn't have far to go." Max helped her rise. "That's good. Now lean on me."

He was steady as a tree trunk, holding her firmly and helping her to stand. She probably could have managed without his assistance, but it felt good to lean on him, to feel his strong arms encircling her. Her vision of the wedding dress had shown her she wasn't quite as independent-minded as she'd thought. That she wasn't, in fact, all that different from Heather in her desire not to spend her life alone. She hadn't wanted Paul, but she still longed to build a life with the right man.

She glanced at the man next to her and her stomach flipped over. Was *Max* the right man?

She tried to push the thought away, but it stayed firmly lodged at the front of her brain. She'd thought being friends with Max was a great idea, but now she realized she'd been fooling herself. She had plenty of female friends if friendship was what she wanted.

For more, she needed a man. A strong, funny, thoughtful, sexy man like Max.

They made their slow, painful way up to the top of the slope, where Hagan immediately unsnapped her from the harness and guided her to lie down on a stiff plastic stretcher. "I'm fine, really," she protested. "I could walk. My shoulder is hurt, not my legs."

"Oh, God, I was so scared," Heather said, hovering beside her. "I feel like such an idiot."

"Unless you pushed her, I can't see why you think that," Hagan said. "You called for help and waited with her. There was nothing else you could do."

Heather was so focused on Casey she didn't even notice that this was one of the longest sentences Hagan had ever directed at her. "This whole thing was my idea. I had this ridiculous plan—"

"I wanted to come on this hike," Casey said, interrupting before Heather could spill a complete confession. "It was my own clumsiness that got me into this. I'm just glad you were here and Hagan and Max arrived so quickly." She managed to catch Heather's gaze and send her a stern look to remind her to keep quiet. Whatever her plan had been, she hadn't gone through with it. No need to embarrass either one of them with that story now.

"Lie down now." Hagan urged her back onto the stretcher. "We can't risk you getting light-headed and falling again."

"Plus, you might have injuries we don't know about yet," Max said.

The sound of someone pounding up the trail made them all turn to look. Ben ran toward them, arriving out of breath. "I came as soon as I could," he said. He looked down at Casey. "How are you doing?"

"I'm fine," she said. "I hurt my shoulder."

"Could be dislocated," Max said.

Ben knelt beside the stretcher and gently prodded along her shoulder blade. "How does it feel?" he asked.

She made a face. "It hurts. Especially if I try to move it."

He nodded. "I'll give you something for the pain. Any drug allergies that you know of? Ever had a bad reaction to pain medication?"

"No." She shook her head.

Ben dug in his pack and took out a pill bottle and a bottle of water. Max held Casey's head while she swallowed the pill and sipped some water. She hadn't realized how thirsty she'd been until the cool liquid slid down her throat. It was all she could do to keep from gulping it all.

Ben capped the water bottle and stood. "You've got the shoulder immobilized. Better leave it until we can get to the clinic and take X-rays." He turned to Heather, who had been standing beside the stretcher, wringing her hands. "Are you okay?" Ben asked.

She nodded, though she looked close to tears.

Ben stood and put his arm around her. "She's going to be fine," he said. "She was lucky to have you here to call for help so quickly."

Hagan and Max buckled Casey onto the stretcher and covered her with a blanket, then started back down the trail at a trot. Heather and Ben followed at a slower pace. Their voices eventually faded as the two men left them behind. "You doing okay?" Max asked at one point.

"Yeah." The pain pill Ben had given her was making her drowsy, though the occasional jolt still sent a stab of pain through her shoulder. "Max?" she said after a while.

"I'm here."

"I'm glad you were the one to come," she said. She didn't want to think of herself as a woman who needed rescuing, but when she did she was glad he'd been her rescuer. With Max she didn't have to worry about any ulterior motive—what he'd expect in repayment for his service or how he thought this would affect his image. Max was her friend—her real friend. And if she had hopes he might one day be more, there was nothing wrong with dreaming, was there?

MAX WAS BREATHING HARD by the time they reached the trailhead and Ben's Suburban. He was out of breath not only from the exertion of the run down the trail with Casey in the Stokes basket, but from fighting the panic that had made his heart beat double-time since the call had come in.

Casey's fallen and she's hurt. Those words had frozen his blood. He'd been on enough bad calls in his years with Search and Rescue to know how awful even a simple misstep in the mountains could end up: broken bones, head injuries, even death. A pleasant morning's outing could turn into a tragedy in a moment.

He'd demanded Heather's phone number from the emergency dispatcher and punched it into his phone as he started his Jeep and headed for the trailhead. In tears, Heather had reported that Casey had fallen. She'd been hard to understand, but Max had gotten out of her that Casey was conscious and talking, maybe with a shoulder injury. His heart had slowed a little, but only when he'd reached Casey and seen for himself that she was alive and whole had he relaxed some, though the aftermath of panic still had him shaky and out of breath.

That and the odd way she'd looked at him back on the trail—as if he was some knight in shining armor who'd rescued her from a fire-breathing dragon. Then she'd gone all dreamy and said that about him being more than a friend. Maybe she'd hit her head after all….

They slid the Stokes into the back of Ben's Suburban. If the situation had been dire, they would have radioed for a real ambulance, but Ben's vehicle would serve to transport Casey to the clinic. Max crawled in beside her; he'd get someone to drive him up to fetch the Jeep later. Heather peered in after him, her face unnaturally white in the dim interior of the vehicle. "Should I come, too?" she asked.

"There's not enough room." Hagan took her arm and pulled her back, then prepared to shut the door. "You will be fine," he told Casey, then to Max. "I'm glad she's okay."

"Yeah. Me, too."

The doors closed and Max reached over and took Casey's hand and squeezed it. She squeezed back, but they didn't say anything. He was having a hard time putting words together right now. His thoughts spun like leaves caught in a whirlpool. He was relieved Casey was going to be all right. And disturbed at how much the thought of her hurt had shaken him. He'd felt…out of control. Not something he ever liked to be.

At the clinic, Ben ushered Casey into the back for X-rays while Max sprawled in a chair and pretended to read a magazine. After a few more minutes, Hagan and Heather arrived. "How is she?" Heather asked. "What does Ben say?"

"I haven't heard yet," Max said.

Heather perched on the edge of the sofa and stared at the door to the back of the clinic as if she could will it to open to reveal Casey, whole and well. Hagan sat beside Max and picked up a magazine.

The door opened and Ben emerged with Casey by his side. She was wearing a new sling and looking a little pale, but she was smiling. "Separated shoulder," Ben said before anyone could speak. He patted Casey's uninjured shoulder. "Not even a terribly bad separation. She'll be sore for a couple of days, but in a few weeks she won't even know it ever happened."

"That's great." Max rose and went to her. "I'd offer to drive you home, but I left my Jeep back at the trail."

"I'll take her home." Heather appeared on Casey's other side. "You go with Hagan to get your Jeep. You can stop by later. What she needs now is rest."

He started to protest, but realized Heather was right. She was in full mother-hen mode now, ushering Casey along and all but clucking at her. Max heard something about "Get you tucked into bed" and "homemade soup" and couldn't help but grin. Casey was in good hands now.

"I'll check in with you later," Ben said, walking with them to the door.

Casey looked up, surprised. "You make house calls?"

Ben grinned. "For a select few."

Max felt a stab of annoyance. If Casey was all right, why did Ben feel it necessary to stop by her apartment and see her? And why was he grinning that way?

Hagan nudged him. "Let's go get your Jeep," he said. "I have to get back to work."

"Yeah. I should do that, too." Get back to work and get

back to his regular life, uncomplicated by wild emotions and confusing situations. Undisturbed by women who fell off cliffs and took pieces of him with them.

Chapter Nine

A week after Casey's accident, Max was in the middle of re-
placing a tire on a bike when his cell phone rang. Not missing
a beat, he grabbed the phone and stuck it between his ear and
shoulder. "Hello."

"Max, this is your mother."

Max checked the clock on the workroom wall. Ten a.m.
mountain time, which meant his mother was calling from her
desk at the family factory during her lunch hour. "Hey, Mom.
How are you?"

"I'm well, thank you. I called to let you know your father
and I are planning a visit."

"A visit?" He frowned. "Where?"

She laughed. "To you! We've been reading about the wonderful Wildflower Festival you have out there and we thought,
why not? We're looking forward to seeing you and the town."

He sat back on his heels and let this information sink in.
His parents. Here? He'd always visited them in their home—
never the other way around. It would be good to see them
again, but he had a hard time picturing them with his friends,
walking these streets, occupying this world he'd made his
own. The one place that was truly his own.

But he couldn't very well tell them that. "That's great, Mom," he said, forcing cheerfulness into his voice. "When are you coming?"

"We're flying out Friday."

Friday? That was three days away. "So soon? I mean, I want time to get everything ready for you." He'd have to clean his apartment, stock up on groceries…and where were they going to sleep? At least all the puppies had gone to their new homes last week. His place had a lot more room now that it was just him and Molly again. But not really enough for his parents.

An apartment over a snowboard shop wasn't exactly their type of place, anyway. His father would feel compelled to give him a lecture on the investment potential of a home and his mother would blanch when she saw the antique plumbing fixtures. The fact that Max loved everything about the place wouldn't matter so much to them.

"Don't worry about a thing," his mother said. "We've made reservations at a bed-and-breakfast there—a place called The Ruby? Do you know anything about it?"

He relaxed a little. "The Ruby is very nice. You'll love it." The Ruby was near the chamber of commerce and catered to people with dogs. "Are you bringing Raffles?" Raffles was an elderly shih tzu who hated everyone but Max's mother.

"Of course, dear. He'll enjoy the trip."

Max doubted the dog's idea of a good time was being stuffed in a carrier and flown across the country, but he didn't bother to point this out.

"I called to give you our flight information," his mother continued. "We're arriving at 2:17 on flight—"

"Hang on, let me grab something to write on." He stood and pawed among the clutter on the workbench until he found a crumpled receipt for an order of shifters and a stubby pencil. "Okay, give me the info."

He scribbled their information, along with his mother's cell number—which he probably already had somewhere, but who knew where—and stuffed the paper into his pocket. "Say hello to Dad," he said. "I'll see you both Friday."

They said goodbye and he clicked off the phone and leaned back against the workbench. His parents. Here. He could hardly believe it.

Zephyr shuffled in, followed by Bryan. Zephyr stopped halfway across the room and took a step back from Max. "Whoa, you eat something that didn't agree with you?" Zephyr asked.

"No, why?"

"You look a little sick or something."

"My mom just called and told me she and my dad are coming to Crested Butte this weekend."

"Your parental units are coming here?" Zephyr grinned. "Sweet! I can't wait to meet them."

Max studied the musician. Today he wore Tevas, salmon-pink cargo shorts and a T-shirt that featured a cartoon bear making an obscene gesture. "I'll have to introduce you," he said. Next to Zephyr, Max would look like a model citizen.

"Have they been here before?" Bryan asked.

Max shook his head. "Nope. This will be a first." He'd never gotten around to inviting them. Not that he didn't love his family—he did and he made it a point to fly back to Connecticut to visit them at least once a year. But he'd built his own life here in C.B., a very different life from the one they'd envisioned for him. Being different had become a point of pride with him, but defending his choices was a lot easier from a distance of almost two thousand miles than facing their disappointment close at hand.

Other than objecting when he dropped out of college, his parents had never openly disapproved of anything he'd done. Instead, they would listen to the latest news of his life in Colorado, nodding and looking sad. One of them, usually his mother, would say something such as, "Well, if that's what you really want to do…." her voice trailing away as if it hurt too much to even finish the sentence. It was a technique guaranteed to make him feel guilty.

"Earth to Max." Zephyr snapped his fingers in front of Max's face. "Don't worry about the folks, dude. Just do what I do when my parents visit."

Zephyr had parents? Of course he did, but Max had never thought about them before. He had a sudden image of an older version of Zephyr—and a Mrs. Zephyr. He suppressed a shudder. "What do you do?" he asked.

"Wear 'em out. Find so many things for them to do while they're here that they don't have time to stop and criticize. And they're glad to leave so they can get some rest."

"Not a bad idea," Bryan said. "But take it easy on the hiking and stuff if they have bad hearts or anything."

Max shoved away from the bench. "Thanks for the ideas, guys," he said. "What can I do for you, Bryan?"

"I need a new brake cable for my ride." Bryan held up a broken cable. "Zeph said he thought you had one back here."

"Yeah, over on that wall." Max pointed toward the far wall where parts were stored in labeled bins. He clapped Zephyr on the shoulder. "Hold down the fort for a while. I'm going over to the chamber."

"Tell Casey and Heather I said hi," Zephyr said.

On the way to the chamber offices, Max started a mental list of things he needed to do, buy or schedule in preparation for his parents' visit. He stopped by the post office to collect the mail—junk, bills and another letter for Casey from that Paul person. Max was tempted to toss it straight into the trash, since she shredded all Paul's letters, anyway, but he tucked it in his pocket with the bills and headed for the chamber offices.

Lucy greeted him at the door, her entire body wiggling. "Are you the official greeter?" he asked, patting her side. The little black dog wasn't so little anymore. She wore a red bandana around her neck and her tags jingled as she followed Max inside.

Casey was standing on a ladder just inside the door, hanging a giant cardboard cutout of a gaillardia blossom. Her shoulder was out of the sling now and though she couldn't lift anything heavy with that arm she said it didn't bother her much. She was wearing a short khaki skirt and her very shapely thighs were right at Max's eye level. He stopped and admired them, grinning.

He'd been playing it cool with her since her accident and neither of them had mentioned the goofy way she'd acted when he'd first found her. She went along with his just-friends manner, but every once in a while he caught her watching him with that dreamy look in her eye—as if she were sizing him up for a tuxedo.

"What are you staring at?" she asked, looking down at him.

"Just enjoying the view." He waggled his eyebrows and leered in a lecherous parody.

She swatted at him and climbed down from the ladder. "What's up?" she asked.

"I brought your mail." He handed her the single envelope.

She looked dismayed, but quickly recovered and headed for her desk. He followed her. Lucy curled up on a dog bed nearby.

"Hey, Max," Heather said as she hung up the phone. She'd recently cut her hair in a short, flattering style and she was wearing more makeup than usual. He wondered if she had a new man in her life. He'd have to ask Casey.

"I actually stopped by because I hope you two can help me," he said.

"Oh?" Casey looked up expectantly.

"Yeah." He sat on the edge of her desk. "My parents are coming to visit and I need ideas for things they can do while they're here. A schedule of activities for the Wildflower Festival, I guess. And maybe some brochures on scenic drives."

"We can help you there." Heather walked to the brochure racks. "We've got concerts. Wildflower walks. Balloon rides. Does your mom or dad fish? I can give you information on fly-fishing outfitters. Backcountry Jeep tours. Self-guided history walks. Black Canyon of the Gunnison National Park...." As she spoke she plucked brochures from the racks.

"Have your parents visited Crested Butte before?" Casey asked.

"No. They don't like to travel much and it's a long way. I usually go to Connecticut instead."

"They picked the perfect time to come," Heather said, in full chamber director mode. "The weather is perfect in July and the flowers make the scenery more spectacular than usual. They'll understand why you came and didn't want to leave."

"I'm not holding my breath on that one," Max said. The Overbridges had lived in Connecticut for five generations, a fact that was mentioned with pride whenever any of their acquaintances talked of moving.

"I'm looking forward to meeting them," Casey said.

Max smiled at her. "They'll love you," he said. Whatever they thought of the other choices he'd made, his parents would have no objection to Casey. She was exactly the sort of beautiful, well-bred woman that they would have chosen for him themselves.

Which made him wonder sometimes why *he* was so attracted to her, since he had a natural aversion to everything else in his parents' lifestyle. Then again, Casey was a rebel like him. She'd left her home in Chicago society and started over in C.B., just as he had.

While Heather arranged brochures, maps and flyers into a Welcome to Crested Butte folder, Casey fed Paul's letter into the shredder. Max waited for the machine to stop whirring, then said. "Why don't you tell him to stop writing?"

"I did, but Paul never believes anything anyone says if it goes against what he's already made up his mind to do."

"Does he send love letters or hate mail?" His tone was casual, but he had an uncomfortable tightness in his chest as he waited for her answer.

"A little of both, I imagine." Her eyes met his and the tightness in his chest increased. Her look held a challenge, as if she were daring him to declare his own feelings for her.

He looked away, not ready to go there yet. He was a take-things-as-they-come kind of guy. When women started expecting a man to talk about his feelings, it was one more step on the road to picking out rings and wedding gowns. The longer he could avoid that with Casey, the better for both of them.

"Here's all kinds of information for you." Heather handed him a fat folder, along with a chamber of commerce pin and a magnet. "There's enough in here to keep your parents entertained for weeks."

"How long are they staying?" Casey asked.

"Uh, I don't know. I didn't ask." He juggled the over-full folder. "I'd better go. I have a lot to do."

"Let me know if there's anything I can do to help," Casey said. "I'll stop by your place after work."

"Yeah. That'd be great. I could use some help." He nodded goodbye and pushed out the door. The sun was as bright as ever, the sky its usual intense blue, but he felt as if one of those cartoon clouds had settled over his head. He had a great life here in C.B. Exactly the life he wanted. He hated the idea that his parents might come here and somehow taint his happiness by reminding him he hadn't lived up to all their expectations for him.

"I WONDER WHAT Max's parents are like," Heather said when Max was gone.

"I'm guessing his dad is an older version of Max," Casey said. She smiled at the thought of Max with a few more lines on his face, a touch of gray in his hair. He'd look even more rugged and handsome than he did now.

"Kind of funny they haven't been out here before," Heather said. "My parents love to visit Crested Butte."

"I don't think my parents would like it," Casey said. "They're real city people." She didn't want to hear her parents find fault with a place she was fast falling in love with.

"I guess everybody's different." Heather tucked a lock of hair behind one ear and began shuffling through the stacks of papers on her desk.

"I like your new haircut," Casey said. "It's really flattering." Not that Heather wouldn't look great in any style.

"Thanks. I wanted a change, so I asked Mica over at Moxie to do something a little more hip." She fluffed her hair. "Even Emma approved."

"What's the latest with you and Hagan?" Heather hadn't mentioned the handsome Norseman since Casey's accident.

Heather made a face. "He'll say more than two words to

me now, but he's not hanging around any more than he did before. I've thrown out lots of hints, but he hasn't asked me to go with him for a drink or a cup of coffee or anything." She shrugged. "I guess you could say I've moved from nonexistent to casual acquaintance. I'm hoping the new look will generate some sparks."

"Or maybe some other hot guy will notice you and you'll forget all about Hagan." Casey returned her attention to the work on her desk. She was trying to compile the schedule of events for the upcoming Arts and Film Festival.

"Speaking of hopeless cases," Heather said. "What are you going to do about Paul?"

"What do you mean?"

"Are you just going to let him keep writing to you like that?" She glanced at the wastebasket. "While you shred his letters?"

"I'm not *letting* him do anything. He does it. I told him to stop."

"But he hasn't." Heather sank into her desk chair. "Doesn't that make you wonder?"

"Yeah, it makes me wonder if he's some kind of stalker." Honestly, Paul had never been so devoted when they were dating. What was he trying to prove by pursuing her so relentlessly now?

"Maybe he really loves you," Heather said. "He refuses to give up." She wore a dreamy expression. "That's very admirable in a man, I think."

"That he won't take no for an answer?" Casey stared at her friend. "You don't think it's creepy?"

"It could be…but he hasn't said anything creepy in the letters, has he? The ones you did read?"

She shook her head. "Paul isn't a creep. He's kind of boring, really. And a little stuffy."

Heather hesitated. "I may be out of line here, but, speaking strictly as a woman who would give almost anything to have a man adore me that way—do you think you made a mistake dumping him?"

"I didn't love him." No mistaking that.

"Okay. I can accept that." Heather picked up a stack of folders and straightened them. "But was it *him* you didn't love—or just the lifestyle he represented? That whole Chicago society, political career and everything that went with it that you told me you wanted to get away from?"

Casey shifted in her chair. "I *did* want to get away from those things, but I didn't love Paul."

Heather nodded. "Okay. I believe you. I just wanted to make sure." Again she glanced toward the wastebasket. "I'm still impressed that he would write you every single week for how many weeks now?"

"Thirteen."

"Thirteen weeks. Even though you haven't answered him. Now that's devotion."

"Or lunacy. I would have thought he'd have more self-respect than that."

"Love trumps self-respect every time," Heather said. "Look at the lengths I've been willing to go to try to attract Hagan. Not that it's done me any good so far." She stapled a stack of forms together. "Maybe Paul and I have a lot in common."

"If he lived closer, I'd offer to fix you up."

"No, I'm stuck on Hagan. It's hopeless." She glanced at Casey. "Again, none of my business, but you'll notice I've never let that stop me before. Are you in love with Max?"

The question startled the breath out of her, so much that for a moment she couldn't speak. "I—I don't know," she finally stammered. "I really like him but...but he's done a pretty good job so far of keeping me at a distance."

"He's like that. He's never going to write you a letter a week or beg you for anything. You might want to think about that."

"I don't need all those things from a man who truly loves me."

"But does Max love you? Has he said so?"

"Not yet. We aren't at that point in our relationship yet. There's no rush." But she didn't want to stay single all her life, either. It was one thing to nod and smile when Max talked about the joys of independence, but personal freedom only took a person so far. When Casey was perfectly honest with herself, she had to admit a woman who really and truly wanted to remain single wouldn't keep a wedding dress in the back of her closet.

MAX'S DAD, Marvin, was indeed an older, stockier version of his son. And Max's mother, Delia, was a tall, angular woman with an avid interest in everything. Their first evening in Crested Butte, Max took them to dinner at Donita's Cantina on Elk Avenue and by unspoken agreement all his friends showed up, so that the wait staff ended up pushing tables together and making a party of it.

Casey was there as Max's date and she had a good view of his face as first Trish, then Bryan and Zephyr, Heather and her daughter Emma, then, finally, Hagan filtered in. As Max made introductions, each friend pulled a chair up to the table, until Mr. and Mrs. Overbridge were surrounded by Max's regular social circle.

Zephyr ended up next to Delia. He'd dressed up for the occasion in a white T-shirt with the outline of a tuxedo on it, complete with cummerbund and bow tie. To this he'd added a checked sport coat worn over khaki shorts. Delia studied him, wide-eyed. "How *do* you get your hair to do that?" she asked after a moment.

"The dreads?" Zephyr fingered one of the fat blond locks. "It's easy."

"I thought only African-Americans could make their hair do that," Delia said.

"Nah. As long as you've got some kink in there, you can do it."

Max choked on his margarita. While his father pounded his back, Zephyr explained to Delia how to lock hair.

"That's very interesting," Delia said, sounding sincere.

"Are you thinking of trying it, Mom?" Max asked.

"No. My hair has always been straight as string, you know that."

Casey caught Max's eye and winked. She leaned close and whispered. "I like your parents."

"The margarita must have loosened her up. My mom isn't usually so easygoing."

"Where are you from originally?" Marvin asked Casey. "Or are you a native Crested Buttian or whatever they're called."

"I'm originally from Chicago," she said. "I've only been here a few months."

Marvin grinned. "I love Chicago. Great city. Ever make it to a White Sox game?"

"A few times." One of Paul's clients had a box and they'd attended periodically. The view from that high wasn't much and it was difficult to pay attention to the game, anyway, when she was expected to smile and mingle and shmooze.

"Do you ski?" Delia asked.

Casey shook her head.

"Snowboard?" Marvin asked.

"No. I'm not very athletic."

"I thought everyone came here for the skiing and other outdoor activities," Marvin said.

"Most people do," she said. "I came because of the job." Which was far from the whole truth. "But I like it here very much," she hastened to add.

"Good thing not everyone is like you, or Max would be out of business," his dad said. He turned to Max. "How is that going?"

"Great, Dad. It's going great." Max swept a chip idly through a bowl of salsa. "I added more rental bikes this year and I got an exclusive agreement with Never Summer to carry their snowboarding gear this winter."

"You ought to be looking for opportunities to expand your space," Marvin said. "There's no room for real growth in the store you're in now. Or maybe you could add a second location. Maybe up at the resort."

"I'm not interested in getting too big," Max said. "The size I am now gives me a good living without being too much of a hassle."

"A little hassle could be worth a lot of money," his dad said. "Your brother George brokered a deal for us to double our warehouse space and it's really paid off. And Miranda is expanding our Web presence. There's no limit to the growth we can handle now."

"You should talk to Miranda about building a Web site," his mother said. "She's a genius and I'm sure she'd make time to help out her little brother."

"That's great, but I don't need her help," Max said, his voice strained.

"There's no reason a larger concern can't run as smoothly as a smaller one," his father continued. "If you need any tips, you know I have all kinds of experience. And, of course, George can tell you anything you need to know."

Max looked as if he'd swallowed something bitter. "Thanks, Dad. I'm happy with things the way they are."

Zephyr, of all people, came to Max's rescue. "Mr. Overbridge, could you hand me that bowl of salsa?" he asked.

"Of course." Marvin handed over the salsa.

"Thanks." Zephyr accepted the bowl. "I just love this stuff." He turned to Delia. "I bet they don't have salsa like this in Connecticut, do they?" he asked.

Delia smiled. "No, they don't."

Casey imagined Max's mother was thinking they didn't have many dreadlocked musicians or bright-pink snowboard shops in Connecticut, either.

Their entrées arrived and conversation lagged as everyone devoted themselves to enchiladas, chili *rellenos* and the other Mexican dishes Donita's was known for. "Did you have a good flight?" Casey asked Marvin after a while.

"As nice as any flight is these days," he said. "I don't care much for travel."

"You couldn't have picked a better time to visit," Heather said. "What do you have planned while you're here?"

"We want to see your famous wildflowers," Delia said. "And we'll probably take a drive out to Black Canyon of the Gunnison. But mainly we wanted to see Max." She smiled at her son. "You're looking well, son."

"The modern mountain man," Marvin declared. He was well into his second margarita and his cheeks were flushed. He was by no means drunk, merely very relaxed.

"Did you know Max volunteers with Search and Rescue?" Casey asked. If Max was worried about his parents' opinion, it couldn't hurt to try to impress them a little.

"No, I didn't know that." Marvin looked at his son, genuinely surprised. "Why didn't you tell us, Max?"

He shifted in his chair and kept his eyes on his plate. "It's no big deal. Mainly finding lost hikers."

"Some of those hikers are at the bottom of deep canyons, or pinned under boulders," Hagan said from the other end of the table. "It sometimes takes a lot of hard work and courage to reach them."

"He rescued me when I fell hiking and hurt my shoulder," Casey said.

"Hagan works with Search and Rescue, too," Heather chimed in. "It's incredible some of the things those men and women do—rappelling down cliffs, climbing mountains... amazing stuff."

Delia looked down the table and for the first time seemed to notice Hagan. "It's very generous of you to volunteer your time that way," she said. Casey could have sworn her eyelashes fluttered. Hagan did tend to have that affect on women.

"It's a good way to meet women," Hagan said with a wink.

Delia *giggled* and Max glared at his friend, while Casey hid her face in her napkin to keep from bursting out laughing.

Finally every plate was clean, every glass empty. Everyone began taking their leave, until only Casey, Max and his parents were left at the table. "It was nice to meet your friends," Delia said. "A very interesting group of young people."

Marvin and Delia stood and Max rose also. "I'll walk you back to the Ruby," he said.

"We can find our own way back. Then we'll need to take Raffles out for his walk." Marvin put his arm around his wife. "We'll drop you and Casey off at your apartments."

The night was warm, and locals and visitors alike lingered

around the shops and restaurants along Elk Avenue. The sounds of music and conversation spilled out from the Eldo. Several people hailed Max and Casey from the crowded balcony as they passed. Max waved, but kept walking.

The foursome stopped in front of Mad Max's. "It was nice meeting you," Delia said to Casey. "I'm sure we'll see more of you this weekend."

"I'm sure. It was great meeting you, too."

"See you tomorrow, son."

"Good night."

After the older couple had walked away, Casey turned to Max. "They really are nice," she said. "And it's obvious they're proud of you."

Max frowned. "Did you hear my dad? It's not enough that I have a successful business. It should be bigger. Better. And, of course, nothing I do will ever compare to my brother and sister's genius."

"They didn't mean it that way. He just…wanted to share what he's learned." She put a hand on his arm. "Pass along his wisdom. Parents do that."

He shook his head. "I don't need his wisdom. I don't want to do things the way he did them. I like doing things on my own."

She locked her arm in his and they started up the stairs. "They were impressed when I told them you work with Search and Rescue," she said. "I'll bet your dad never did anything like that."

"I'm sure if he'd had more time and fewer margaritas he would have thought of some criticism."

She refused to let his pessimism mar her impression of the evening. "They're just normal parents," she said. "And they really do love you."

"I know they love me. But they don't approve of me."

She wanted to shake him. Would it kill him to look on the bright side of things? They stopped in front of the door to her apartment. "Try to enjoy their visit," she said. "They'll be gone soon enough."

He nodded and patted her arm. "Thanks for being there tonight," he said. "They really liked you."

"And I like you. A lot."

He kissed her good night. What he'd lacked in enthusiasm for the evening, he made up for in that kiss. "Maybe I should come in for a while," he said when they finally parted.

It was tempting, but she knew if she invited him in, he wouldn't be going home and she didn't think now was a good time to take that next step. Not while his emotions were so stirred up by his parents' presence. "We both have stuff to do tomorrow," she said. "And you have to play host to your parents." She kissed his cheek. "But I'll take a rain check."

For a moment his eyes met hers, his gaze penetrating. "It rains every afternoon here in late summer," he said.

"Mmm." She smiled. "Then I'll have plenty of opportunities to collect what I'm due, won't I?"

He pulled her close and kissed her again, a fierce, quick embrace. "I'm hoping for a downpour—very soon." Then he retreated across the hall and through his own door, as if he needed the extra barrier between them.

She sagged against the wall, out of breath. Max was definitely a difficult man to resist. Heather's question of a few days before echoed in her head. *Do you love him?*

A better question might be, how could she not love him? He was a lovable guy and she was a woman with an open heart, just waiting for the right man to walk in.

Chapter Ten

Max took his parents to the airport Monday afternoon. They had appeared to enjoy their trip, taking in all the local sights and leaving with a memory card full of photographs, two Crested Butte sweatshirts and some local artwork. Spending time with them—and seeing how different they were from the way Max had portrayed them, made Casey wonder if she'd misjudged her own parents. Maybe this distance from them would give her a new perspective that would enable her to have a better relationship with them in the future.

When she got home from work Monday, she called Chicago. Her mother answered, obviously surprised to hear from her, which made Casey feel even guiltier. "Hi, Mom. How are things there?" she asked, trying for cheerful, but afraid she was coming across as manic.

"I'm dressing for a fund-raising dinner for the Chicago Arts League. The mayor's last term is up in two years and your father is considering running for the office, so it's never too soon to start campaigning."

Casey said a silent prayer of thanks that she'd moved when she did. When her father had previously campaigned for public office, she'd been dressed up and put on display at every opportunity. She'd been expected to shake hands, make small talk and extol her father's virtues at endless dinners, rallies and other meetings. Every word that came out of her mouth had been coached and rehearsed. She'd felt like a robot. Her parents might have ordered her from a catalog— "The perfect political daughter."

"I hope you'll be back home by the time he announces his candidacy," her mother continued. "It would look good to have the whole family around him."

Casey checked her watch. Less than a minute into the conversation and the lecture was starting. Mom was showing a lot of restraint these days. "Mom, I'm not moving back home. I like it here." She sat in a kitchen chair and Lucy ran to her. Casey caressed the dog's soft ears as she listened to her mother.

"Your home is here. And Paul is here. He says he's been writing to you."

Casey twisted the phone cord around her wrist and made a face. "Tell him to stop. I've asked him to and he won't listen to me."

"He knows a wonderful therapist you should talk to."

"A therapist! Mom, I don't need a therapist. Do you think I'm crazy?"

"Not crazy, but…what do you call it when a young woman walks away from marriage to a man who is absolutely perfect for her, who leaves a wonderful apartment and a great job to go live over a snowboard shop in a tiny mountain town, doing work that doesn't begin to utilize her talents? Not to mention you're not making half of what you made here."

Casey struggled not to come across as defensive, even while she defended her choices. "I enjoy my work with the chamber," she said. "And I make plenty to support myself."

"It's not too late to come home and salvage your reputation. Paul is willing to go through with the wedding—though we'd make it a smaller affair this time, of course. Something here at home. You still have the dress, I suppose."

She didn't want to talk about the dress. She didn't want to talk about any of this. "Where is the dinner tonight being held?" she asked.

"The Hilton. Sharon Elsberg is in charge of the arrangements—a completely uninspired choice. You would have done a much better job. If you'd stayed home you could have had the position, I'm sure."

Casey bit the inside of her cheek to keep from groaning. The relentless focus that made her mom such a good organizer and political wife made it almost impossible to win any debate with her. "I'd better let you finish getting ready for the dinner," she said. "I just wanted to call and say hello."

"Yes, your father will be home soon and we have to leave for dinner right away. I'll say hello to Paul for you."

"Mother!"

But her mother had already hung up. Casey slumped in her chair and stared at the pattern of roses in the rug. She didn't know which bothered her more—the fact that her mother had not asked a single question about how Casey was doing or the knowledge that her parents wouldn't listen to or acknowledge her opinions regarding her own life. She was living on her own, supporting herself, but to them she might as well have been six years old, still needing Mommy and Daddy to make all her decisions for her.

She sat up straighter and took a deep breath. Pouting about this wasn't exactly mature behavior. Time to think like an adult. Maybe her parents only wanted the best for her. Maybe to them she did seem crazy.

She looked around her apartment, which was warm and

cozy, furnished with well-used antiques. Lucy's toys were scattered around the rug; at the moment the dog was stretched out on the floor, chewing a piece of rawhide.

This place had none of the plushness or designer details of her Chicago residence, which had had twice the space and cost four times the rent. And owning a dog would have been out of the question there. Casey didn't miss the luxury she'd left behind, but her mother would no doubt be appalled to see this place. Knowing it was situated over a snowboard shop had been enough to make her shudder.

In Chicago, Casey had been a junior executive at one of the top marketing firms. She'd been part of a team that had handled several big accounts. The work had been challenging, but the office atmosphere had been cutthroat and stressful. All her coworkers seemed determined to get ahead by climbing on the backs of their fellow employees. The job had paid well—twice her current salary—but she had never looked forward to going to work there as she did in Crested Butte.

Her mom no doubt thought Casey was sacrificing her opportunity to have a vibrant social life. In Chicago, her evenings and weekends had been filled with parties, dinners and performances of the theater, symphony and ballet. She often went out on the town with groups of men and women she'd known most of her life. But she never felt close to them, not as close as she felt now to Heather, Trish, Max and so many other new friends she'd made.

Then there was the matter of boyfriends. Her mother had always held up Paul as the ideal catch—good-looking, successful, wealthy, with all the right social connections and the promise of a shining political career ahead of him. Many of the young women Casey knew agreed. If asked to choose between Paul and a shaggy-haired snowboarder who ran a small business and lived in an apartment above his shop, a man who preferred a mountain bike to a Miata and who probably didn't even own a suit, much less one with a designer label, they all would have laughed and assumed she was joking.

Casey agreed there was no comparison between the two. To her, Max was infinitely more interesting. In his company, she could truly be herself, with no expectations—no role to fill or image to convey. Max worked hard, played hard, took good care of Molly and her puppies and was loyal to his friends. He was a strong man people knew they could depend on. No amount of money in the bank could buy those qualities.

Restless, she went to the closet and pulled out the garment bag that held the wedding dress. Maybe it was time she got rid of this. It was part of her past—a reminder of misplaced dreams and mistakes.

She pulled down the zipper and a froth of off-white satin and lace spilled forth, like foam overflowing from a shaken soda. The dress had a sweetheart neckline and a fitted bodice covered with lace and hundreds of tiny glass beads. Full, shear sleeves ended in banded cuffs fastened with pearl buttons. The skirt billowed out from the waist, with two stiff petticoats beneath it accentuating the fullness.

Casey had loved the dress the moment she had seen it in the bridal boutique. It had an old-fashioned flavor and wearing it made her feel like a princess. Her mother had rejected it immediately. She wanted something more modern, preferably with a designer label. No doubt she was already picturing the write-up of the wedding in the *Chicago Tribune*. *The bride, daughter of mayoral adviser Charles Jernigan and his wife, Ada Jernigan, president of the League of Women*

Voters of Chicago and chair of the mayor's education task force, wore a striking Vera Wang gown of white peau de soie, *trimmed with ostrich feathers and pearls.*

Casey had allowed her mother to dictate every other aspect of the wedding, but she refused to give in on the matter of the dress. "It's my wedding and this is the dress I want," she'd declared and never backed down.

"It's not like you to be so stubborn," her mother had said, shortly before giving in and ordering the dress.

That first victory gave Casey the courage she needed to refuse to go through with a marriage she knew in her heart was wrong. From then on every other decision—from quitting her job to moving to Crested Butte—had seemed easier and easier.

Impulsively, she pulled her T-shirt over her head and stepped out of her jeans, then slid carefully into the dress. Even without the formfitting undergarments she'd worn on her wedding day, the dress fit well. The satin was cool and smooth against her skin, the boned bodice hugging her curves.

Gathering the skirt carefully to hold it off the floor, she tiptoed into the bathroom, the petticoats rustling as if she were walking through piles of dried leaves. On the back of the door was a full-length mirror and she admired her reflection. Her cheeks were flushed, her hair a wild tangle around her shoulders, but she thought she looked pretty. Certainly more relaxed and content than she had the day she was to have married Paul. Then, her eyes had been red-rimmed from crying and shadowed with dark circles. Her smile had been pinched and even with makeup she'd been as pale as someone suffering from a long illness.

She smoothed her hand down the bodice, the beads and lace rough against her palm. She still loved the dress—not for what it had been, but for what it represented. The first time she'd seen the gown in the bridal shop, it had spoke to her of the happily-ever-after of fairy tales. She wanted that dream for herself, and though she hadn't found it yet, she was convinced that it was still possible. One day, she would marry a man she loved. She would wear this dress and see its promise fulfilled.

MAX DROVE HOME from the airport late Monday afternoon feeling pleased about his parents' visit. The weekend had gone better than he'd expected. He'd gotten good at tuning out the references to his older brother and sister's successes, and had managed to bite his tongue and keep quiet about any criticism of himself.

There had been some really good moments, too. Saturday afternoon, while his mother shopped, Max and his dad had climbed a couple of miles into the mountains and eaten lunch overlooking a clear, cold stream. Neither of them had said much, but Max had felt a warm companionship that formed a lump in his throat even now as he remembered the moment.

And last night, he and Casey had shared dinner with his parents at The Buffalo Grill. They'd laughed and reminisced and he couldn't remember when he'd been more relaxed. Maybe their relationship was shifting now that he was grown.

Or maybe he should give Casey all the credit. She'd kept him grounded in the present, not tied to the past, where he was always the screwup youngest kid. She continually reminded him of all he had going for him in his life right now. Whenever his dad talked about things Max should do to improve his business or himself, Casey would reach under the table, squeeze his hand and give him a look that said *she* was proud of him just the way he was.

He had really lucked out the day she came to town. Being with her made him feel better about everything. He wasn't like Hagan, a love 'em and leave 'em kind of guy. Max liked knowing a woman was there for him, that they could have a real relationship that deepened over time.

And he thought Casey wanted that, too. She was happy to be on her own for the first time, building her own life, in no hurry to be tied down, but wanting to be with him.

Lately, he wanted to be with her more and more. She was a special woman and made him feel things he hadn't allowed himself to feel in a long time. Maybe he was even falling in love with her. The idea made him a little nervous, but he told himself he had plenty of time to get used to the idea before he said anything to Casey. He could prepare himself for the dreamy looks the news would no doubt engender.

It started raining as he pulled into town, and he grinned. He parked the Jeep, took the stairs up to the apartments two at a time and rapped hard on Casey's door.

"Max!" Her smile made his heart beat faster and her joy at seeing him did funny things to his stomach. "Did your parents get to their flight all right?" she asked.

"They did." He pulled a bottle of wine from behind his back. "Want to help me celebrate? Mom helped me pick this out. She says it's good."

She held the door wider and motioned for him to come in. He shut the door behind him and set the bottle of wine on a table, then pulled her to him and kissed her, an urgent, hungry kiss.

She responded warmly, easing her arms around him and hugging him tightly. "You *are* in a good mood," she said when they parted.

"It's raining," he said.

She smiled. "Yes, it is."

They kissed again, a lingering caress. The scent of rain coming through the open window mingled with the green-apple fragrance of her shampoo. Max nuzzled her neck. "I'll never look at apple pie the same again," he murmured.

She laughed. "Why is that?"

"You smell like apples." He smoothed one hand down her hip and pressed her closer, enjoying the way her body shaped to his, curves and hollows fitting together so well. "I realized something this weekend," he said.

She leaned back to look up at him. "What's that?"

"I realized I love you." He honestly hadn't meant to say the words, but they'd just popped out. With other women, the words had been hard to say. With some, he had never said them, never felt what he felt for Casey. With her the words came easily, as if holding them in would be denying himself some great pleasure.

A blush warmed her cheeks and her eyes glowed with an inner light. "I love you, too," she said softly, her fingers caressing the back of his neck.

They kissed again, as if to seal the words. She arched against him and he slid one hand down to cover her breast, resting there a moment, feeling her heart beat, her nipple bead against his palm. "I want to make love to you," he said.

Her answer was a smile and a nod. "Let's go into the bedroom," she said, then took his hand and led him toward the antique iron bed. He closed the door behind them, shutting out Lucy, who whined for a few seconds, then sank heavily to the floor in the hall. Casey laughed. "Her feelings are hurt."

"She'll get over it."

They stood on either side of the bed and undressed, slowly, almost shyly, then met in the middle of the mattress, moving into each other's arms.

Being with Max was everything Casey had imagined, and many things she had not. She had expected to be aroused by the sight of his naked body. He was lean and muscular. But she had not anticipated how *cherished* she would feel in his arms. Or how close it was possible to feel to another person even when neither said a word.

But, of course, there were things that needed to be said. "Max, you didn't happen to bring a condom with you, did you?" she asked.

He raised his head, frowning. "No. I have some in my apartment…." He looked toward the door. Though it was only across the hall, his bedroom might have been miles away.

"That's all right. I think I have some in my bathroom." She nudged him aside, then padded into the bathroom and rummaged through the box of things she'd never gotten around to unpacking. Near the bottom was a hot-pink makeup bag that had been a gift at one of her wedding showers. She'd blushed furiously and her guests had screamed with laughter when she'd pulled out the candy panties, lewd chocolates, flavored massage oil and other items in the bag. But now she was grateful for the handful of neon-colored condoms she took back to the bedroom.

"I see you're an optimist," Max said, eyeing the half-dozen packages.

"I'm sure you'll exceed my expectations," she said, winking at him.

Whether he took this as a challenge or whether he was always an exceptional lover, she couldn't say. But Max made love to her with a tenderness and passion that put her former fantasies to shame. What should have been awkwardness was replaced by playfulness. Deep kisses mixed with playful pecks, intense strokes with gentle caresses. Casey, who had always doubted her own skill in bed, felt more womanly and sensuous than ever with Max. Everything she did pleased him and he encouraged her every touch and movement with whispered endearments and an exploration of her body that made her believe he intended to know her as fully as possible.

When at last she lay back and guided him into her, every physical and emotional sensation was focused on her need for him. And when her climax came she truly felt as if she were flying in his arms, more complete with him than she had ever been alone.

And later, when he'd found his own release and lay with his head on her breast, she stroked his hair and listened to his breathing in time with the rain against the windowsill. She thought she had never been as happy as she was right now, with this man and with herself.

CASEY WOKE UP LATER, cold. The bedroom window was open a few inches and a chilly breeze flowed over the bed, bringing with it the smell of rain-washed sage. She groped for more covers, but Max was hogging the blankets, rolled up as tight as a burrito.

She tugged at the covers and he stirred. "What's wrong?" he mumbled, groggy.

"I'm cold. You stole the covers."

He rolled over to face her and smiled, a sleepy smile, eyes heavy-lidded and incredibly sexy. Desire tickled her stomach, warring with sleep. "I'll get another blanket," he said, easing into a sitting position. "Where is it?"

"In the closet. But I can get it."

"No, you stay in bed." He threw back the covers and made his way to the closet. She lay back and watched him, smiling.

He was naked and gorgeous, the gray light coming through the window shadowing every muscle, reminding her of statues of Greek athletes she'd seen in the Art Institute of Chicago.

He groped in the closet for a moment, then pulled the chain for the closet light. The groping stopped. In fact, he was entirely *too* still. She sat up. "Max? Did you find the blanket? It's on the top shelf."

He emerged, not with the blanket, but with his arms full of white lace and satin. Casey felt as if she were choking on ice. She'd neglected to place the dress back in the garment bag after she'd tried it on this afternoon.

"What is this?" he asked. His expression was dazed.

Casey felt sick. She tried to swallow, but couldn't. "It's a wedding gown," she said, her voice sounding as if she spoke under water.

He stared down at the dress in his arms. "Why do you have a wedding gown in your closet?"

"It's a long story."

He tossed the dress across the back of a chair, then crossed to the bed and sat. He picked up his jeans from the floor and started putting them on.

"What are you doing?" Casey asked, alarmed.

"I'm getting dressed. Then you're going to tell me your long story."

She gathered the covers around her and watched him, trying to convince herself this was no big deal. It was just a dress. But it was a dress that represented a lot and Max's stiff back and rigid shoulders told her he wasn't happy with whatever he thought the dress revealed about her.

"You remember Paul," she began when he turned to face her.

His expression darkened. "How could I forget him?"

She looked down and plucked at the quilt, as if she could pull the right words from the patterned fabric. "Well, he and I were engaged…."

"Engaged? You never told me that."

She looked up, managing to keep her voice even. "I didn't think it was important."

"You didn't think it was important that you have a fiancé and neglected to tell me?"

"*Had* a fiancé. I broke up with him before I left Chicago." She frowned. "You're blowing this all out of proportion."

"Well, excuse me." He ran one hand across his face. "I'm a little rattled, okay?"

She nodded. "Okay. But calm down. This is no big deal, really."

He took a deep breath and rested his hands on his thighs. "So you broke up with this guy, but he writes you, anyway." His eyes met hers. "He writes you a lot."

"I told him not to. I wish he'd stop."

He looked away, toward the dress. It lay across the chair near the closet, the skirt trailing the floor, arms hanging down, almost like a body. "So you were engaged long enough for you to buy a dress," he said.

"Yes." She knotted the sheet in her hand. She didn't want to tell him the truth, but there was no getting around it. After all, Heather knew. Max had a right to know also. "We'd planned a big wedding. High society and all that. It was ridiculous."

"If you broke the engagement, why did you keep the dress?"

"It's a beautiful dress. And I only got to wear it for a few hours."

"You wore the dress? As in, at a *wedding?*" His voice rose. "You *married* the guy?"

"No, I didn't marry him. I called off the wedding before we said our vows."

His fingers dug into his thighs, and he looked as if he was having trouble breathing. "Let me get this straight. You left the guy at the altar?"

"He wasn't actually at the altar. He was in a side room with his groomsmen. I told him I couldn't go through with it."

He stared at her, as if she was someone he didn't know. Someone he wasn't sure he wanted to know.

"I know it was an awful thing to do," she said. "I felt horrible about it. But that was better than feeling horrible about a marriage. I returned his ring and all the wedding gifts and wrote letters of apology to all the guests."

"And then you left town."

"Yes. I got the job at the chamber and came out here to start over. You already know that part."

"And you brought the dress with you. Why?"

She followed his gaze to the gown. It looked sad lying there. Discarded. She felt almost as if she herself had been cast aside. "It's a beautiful dress," she said again. "The kind I've always wanted. My mother hated it—it was the only thing in the whole wedding I got my way about. I knew if I left it behind she'd give it away or sell it or something. It seemed such a waste."

"And if you happened to find a husband out here it would come in handy."

"Yes. I mean, no!" She glared at him. "I didn't come out here searching for a husband."

"But you're not opposed to the idea."

She raised her chin. "No, I'm not. Of course I want to marry someday. I want to have a family. There's nothing wrong with that."

"But you were okay when I talked about us keeping things casual, just being friends."

His words made her sad. "You said you loved me. Doesn't that change anything?"

"It doesn't mean I'm ready to get married." He stood, as if needing to put even more distance between them.

"And I never said I expected that."

"But you have a dress. That seems pretty ready to me."

Her patience was wearing thin. It was if he *wanted* to think the worst of her motives. "Oh, please. You act as if marriage were a fatal disease. What is so wrong with two people who love each other deciding to spend their lives together? It's normal for people to do that."

"Then I'm not normal." He stood and reached for his shirt. "I don't want to *be* normal. And I don't like being lied to."

Anger propelled her out of the bed. She gathered the sheet and quilt around her and faced him. She was tempted to try to slap some sense into him, but that would mean letting go of the covers and she'd be at even more of a disadvantage naked. "I did not lie to you," she said. "My having that dress or having been engaged before has nothing to do with the two of us."

"Then maybe you lied to yourself." He pulled on the shirt and scowled at her. "Because a woman who carts a dress like that halfway across the country has marriage in the back of her mind, whether she'll admit it or not." He picked up his shoes and started for the door. "I'm leaving."

She watched him go, feeling sick and angry. She wasn't going to apologize. She'd done nothing wrong. *He* was the one who was wrong—so concerned with an idea—an image of himself as the rebel black sheep, that he couldn't see what was right in front of him.

He'd said he loved her. She'd believed he was telling the truth, believed it still after their lovemaking.

And she loved him. In spite of his stubbornness. But that love wasn't going to do anything to ease her heartache. One thing she knew by now was that Max was a very stubborn man. If his fear of commitment was stronger than his love for her, then there was no hope.

Chapter Eleven

Heather took one look at Casey when she and Lucy shuffled into work Tuesday morning and immediately routed the phones to the answering machine and poured two cups of coffee. "Tell me what happened," she said, pulling her chair up to Casey's desk. "I promise to sympathize and help you plot revenge—or figure out a way to knock some sense into Max's head."

Casey stirred sweetener into her cup. She was exhausted, having spent most of the previous night pacing the floor, thinking of all the things she should have said to Max. "Max and I had a fight," she said.

"So I heard. If it's any consolation, he looks worse than you do."

"You've seen him?" She studied Heather's face. "I haven't laid eyes on him since he stormed out of my place in the middle of the night. Zephyr's running the shop today."

"He straggled into the coffee shop on his way out of town this morning. He said he was going backpacking." Heather shook her head. "He reminded me of a big old bear, retreating to the woods to lick his wounds. What happened?"

"He found the wedding dress in my closet."

"You have a wedding dress in your closet?"

She nodded. "It's the one I wore to marry Paul. Only, since we never actually *got* married, I wanted to save it. I mean, it's a gorgeous dress and I hope I need it one day."

"And Max thought you were saving it for him and freaked?"

"Something like that. I tried to explain to him that owning a dress did not mean that I was on the prowl for an immediate groom, but he wouldn't listen. He freaked—as if he thought I'd try to march him down to the justice of the peace that second."

Heather sat back and sighed. "He's an idiot."

"Yeah." But an idiot she still loved, which only made things worse.

"How are you doing with this?" Heather asked.

"Not so great. I mean, part of me is angry with him for being so stupid. And the rest of me is really hurt." She blinked back tears, determined not to waste any more time crying over Max. "We spent the night together for the first time last night. He told me he loved me."

"Oh, sweetie." Heather leaned over and gave Casey a hug. "He really *is* an idiot."

Casey sniffed and nodded, then sat up straight. "I just don't understand why he reacted the way he did. I never said anything to indicate I expected him to propose or anything. It's just a nice, expensive dress I didn't want to throw away."

"That's what it is to you, but to him I guess it was like finding a preacher with a set of rings waiting outside your door."

"Why would I want to marry someone who isn't interested in marrying me?" Casey said.

"Why do I keep trying to catch Hagan's attention?" Heather picked up her coffee cup and sipped. "Emotions aren't always rational."

"He's the one behaving irrationally this time."

"Yeah. It really doesn't sound like Max. He's usually pretty easygoing. Except…" She pursed her lips and fell silent.

"Except what?" Casey asked.

"Max is easygoing, except when something really matters to him. Like when he rescued the dog he had before Molly."

"When people started calling him Mad Max?"

Heather nodded. "Maybe he reacted so strongly to seeing the dress because he senses you're the one woman who might make him break his keep-things-casual rule."

"Right. He left because he loves me so much. Even Max isn't that twisted."

"Wait a minute, now. Think about it. You'd just spent the night together. He told you he loved you. That's a big step for most people—especially most men. He was probably feeling really great about being with you, thinking how perfect everything was and then this dress pops out at him. Like an omen or something. And he realizes he's been a little *too* content for somebody who's serious about staying unattached. That, in fact, he's already attached, at least emotionally."

Casey stared at her friend. Heather almost made sense. Almost. "So what do you think will happen next? Will he come to his senses or decide he's better off without me?"

"What do you think? Do you think he meant it when he said he loved you?"

Casey nodded. "I think he meant it."

"And do you love him? Enough to take him back?"

"Yes."

"Then we'll make sure you get him back. All we have to do is help him realize what he's missing."

"How are we going to do that?"

"The Arts and Film Festival is coming up in August. There's a big party at the Center for the Arts—a costume ball."

Of course. Was there any other kind in C.B.? "How is that going to help me?"

"We'll come up with a costume that's sure to get his attention. Something he won't be able to resist."

Casey shook her head. "There's no such costume. Not to mention I don't want to look desperate, angling for him that way." The way Heather looked around Hagan sometimes, though Casey would never hurt her friend's feelings by saying so.

"Maybe it's better this happened now, before I actually had decided I wanted to marry him," she said, not really convinced. The moment she'd told Max she loved him and had welcomed him into her bed, part of her had started thinking about being with him forever. It wasn't something she would have said out loud so soon, but the pain she felt upon his leaving told her Max had very quickly become much more to her than a temporary boyfriend to keep her company while she got her life on track. Nothing about her feelings for Max felt temporary and the hurt she felt now was bound to linger for a long time. "I don't want to talk about this anymore," she said. She punched the switch to boot up her computer. "What do we need to do today?"

Heather gave her hard look, then shrugged and wheeled her chair back to her own desk. "Call the printer about the posters and banners for the Arts and Film Festival and double-check the film entries. If you need help, we can call Emma in later."

"That's all right," Casey said. "I'm sure a teenager has much better ways to spend a summer day."

"No, she doesn't. She's grounded." Heather frowned. "She wanted to go on an overnight camping trip with a bunch of friends. Girls and boys. No adults. I told her she was crazy. Then she accused me of not trusting her. I told her she was right and the conversation went downhill from there." Heather stapled a sheaf of papers together. "I don't know what's wrong with the girl. I swear I was never so difficult when I was a child. I wonder if she'd behave any better if there were a man in the house—a father figure to help keep her in line."

Casey didn't think Hagan qualified as anyone's idea of a *father figure* but she didn't say anything. "You're doing a good job with Emma," she said. "Some children are just more independent, I guess." Casey herself had been just the opposite—too complacent during her teenage years and beyond. How much better off would she be now if she'd had the courage to rebel more?

AFTER SPENDING THE NIGHT in the woods, Max rose before dawn on Wednesday, packed up camp, then picked the roughest trail he could find and began hiking, reasoning that if he punished his body enough physically, his mind would stop dwelling on Casey. He hadn't slept well the night before, was unable to get comfortable in his sleeping bag. When he did drift off, he dreamed of Casey—lying in his arms, smiling up at him—before he saw her standing in her wedding dress, motioning for him to join her at the front of the church.

He woke in a cold sweat, cursing himself for going off on her the way he had. She probably thought he was insane, pitching such a fit over a dress.

But it had freaked him out to discover there was so much he didn't know about her when he'd been feeling things were so right between them. She'd been engaged to this guy Paul and had left him at the altar—and hadn't thought it important enough to tell him about. If she'd told him the whole story before and offered it up as proof of why she was as reluctant as he was to say "I do," he would have believed her. He'd have been thrilled.

But to hear the story after learning she'd not only saved the dress, but hauled it all the way across the country... What was he supposed to think but that she was prepared for another wedding at the first opportunity and that he was her prime candidate to be the groom?

Even now, she was probably sitting with Heather or Trish and calling him an idiot. Every woman did, eventually. They said he was afraid of commitment. Or immature. Or contrary for no reason. He'd never make them see things the way he saw them.

Maybe they'd understand if they'd grown up the way he had—the youngest in a family with a perfect older brother and sister, not to mention perfect parents. His brother and sister were the best at anything they tried—varsity basketball, valedictorian of the class, academic scholarships to Ivy League schools. And the achievements hadn't stopped when they'd left home. His brother, George, was a brilliant businessman who'd helped grow the family business, married to a woman who was a successful attorney, with two children who showed every sign of being as brilliant as their parents. His sister, Miranda, had married a university professor and produced twin girls who'd already been featured modeling baby clothes in ads for a regional department store.

Max was the only screwup in the lot—the kid who had to repeat first grade and third grade because he couldn't read. He'd been good at sports, but half the time his grades kept him off the team. By the time he was in junior high his records were full of labels—dyslexic, ADHD, learning disabled. To him they all translated as dummy. When he was a kid, he'd tried plenty of times to be like his older siblings and every time he'd failed.

He'd told Casey he'd dropped out of college to be a ski bum, but the truth was he'd been failing. By then he'd decided that the only way to compete with his siblings was to stop trying. His educational achievements would never match their Ivy League diplomas, so he'd dropped out. They had prestigious careers—he'd found work he enjoyed that didn't require him to wear a suit and tie or live up to anyone else's definition of success.

His brother and sister had perfect marriages with children who were prodigies—he wouldn't marry or have a family at all. His friends would be his family and no woman would ever have to compete for his parents' approval the way he had.

He picked up a stick and threw it. Molly bounded after it. Now that her pups were grown and she'd been spayed, she was growing sleek and energetic again.

Faint strains of music sounded, out of place in the silence of the wilderness. It took Max a moment to realize the sound was coming from his cell phone.

Grumbling, he stopped and slung his pack off his shoulder and retrieved the phone from an outside pocket. "Hello?" he barked.

"Where are you?" Hagan demanded.

"Who wants to know?"

"Heather's girl is missing. Heather thinks she took off by herself, intending to meet up with friends camped near Mirror Lake. She left sometime yesterday, didn't come home last night and never showed up at the campsite. Search and Rescue's been called in."

Max's irritation vanished. "I'm not far from there. I'm on the Timberline trail."

He heard the rustle of paper and pictured Hagan consulting a map. "A bunch of us are heading to the trailhead right now."

"I can be there in twenty minutes. Maybe less." As he talked, he shrugged into the pack and started back down the trail at a jog. Molly raced ahead of him. "What was she doing by herself?" he asked. "Did her friends go off and leave her?"

"Heather had told her she couldn't go, so the friends left without her. Apparently after Heather left for work yesterday morning, Emma headed out on her own. When Heather got in from a meeting last night, Emma was missing. None of her friends have seen her."

Max swore under his breath. "I'll meet you there," he said, and snapped shut the phone. Anything could happen to a kid by herself in that rough country. One wrong turn and she could lose the trail and not be found for days. Hikers had disappeared in these mountains and never been found.

"WHEN WE FIND HER, I'm going to hug her so hard I'm liable to crack ribs," Heather told Casey as they raced in Casey's RAV4 toward the Timberline trailhead as the sun transformed the sky from gray to pink and orange. "And then I'm going to ground her until she's twenty-one."

"After this I'm betting she won't do anything so foolish for a very long time," Casey said.

"I hope not." Heather twisted her hands together and leaned forward, as if she could will the vehicle to arrive at the trailhead faster. "I just hope she's all right."

"She will be." Casey reached over and grabbed her hand and squeezed. "You know these Search and Rescue guys are the best."

"Hagan was so sweet. He called and talked to me himself." She laughed, a bitter sound. "It was probably the longest conversation the two of us ever had, and I was too upset to really enjoy it." She glanced at Casey. "He said he thought Max might be hiking in that area. He was going to try to call him and have him meet the team."

Casey nodded, her mouth compressed into a tight line. She wasn't thrilled at the idea of seeing Max now, after the ridiculous way he'd run out on her over something as stupid as a dress she'd saved. Yet part of her missed him so much. In only a few months, he'd become an important part of her days—of her *life*.

The parking lot at the trailhead was packed with Search and Rescue team members' vehicles. Men and women shouldered backpacks, consulted maps and checked radios. Hagan met Heather and Casey at their car. "I reached Max and he's already gone up the trail," he said. "It's a less steep route and the one we think she's most likely to have taken. We talked to one of the boys she was supposed to meet and that's the route they took in."

Casey followed his gaze toward a quartet of young people who huddled on the edge of the parking lot. They were all ordinary-looking kids. They had no business being out here without a parent, but she believed they'd meant no harm.

Margie joined them, her eyes red, as if she'd been crying. This was her day off from the chamber and Casey was touched that she'd be here for the search. "I feel so awful," Margie said. "I'm the one who gave Emma a ride to the trailhead."

"You did?" Heather asked. "When?"

"About ten o'clock yesterday morning. She called and asked if I could give her a ride. She said you were having car trouble so you couldn't take her."

Heather shook her head. "I'm sorry she conned you into that," she said. "You had no way of knowing she was lying."

Margie chewed her thumbnail and sniffed. "I told her I

didn't think she should go hiking by herself like that, but she said you knew and that it was all right."

Heather sighed. "I hate to think what other stories she's told that I know nothing about."

A truck pulled into the parking lot and Ben got out and jogged up to meet them. "How are you doing, Heather?" he asked. "I got here as soon as I could."

"I'm hanging in there," she said. She sounded surprisingly calm to Casey. She was probably in shock.

Ben put a hand on Heather's shoulder briefly. "We're going to find her. Almost everyone here knows Emma and we all want her found as much as you do."

Heather nodded. "What can I do?" she asked. "Should I go with some of the searchers?"

"Not right now," Hagan said. "Stay here at the trailhead. We'll be in touch by radio." He turned to Ben. "Come with me. We're going to head up the trail toward the lake."

More cars arrived and more volunteers bailed out. Bryan came over and hugged Heather. Zephyr was with him. "I closed up the store," he told them. "I figured Max would understand and I was a wreck waiting around there, wondering what was happening here."

Heather smiled at him. "Thanks. You're a real friend."

She and Casey watched as the searchers formed groups, then dispersed in different directions. They were left in the parking lot with the incident commander, Mike; two emergency medical techs and a representative from the sheriff's department who was talking to a reporter. "With so many people searching, they'll find her soon," Casey said.

Heather nodded. "It's nice to know so many people here know her," she said. "She'll be more comfortable with friends than strangers."

"Everyone here is like a member of her extended family," Casey said. "I knew dozens of people in Chicago, but I never felt as close to any of them as I do to my friends here."

Heather nodded. "Everyone here is related, even if not by blood. It really is like being part of a great big family." She didn't add that the most important member of *her* family was missing. Casey took her friend's hand and squeezed it, sending up a silent prayer that Emma would be found alive and well, and soon.

CASEY COULDN'T REMEMBER another day that had been so long. She sat with Heather in the trailhead parking lot hour after hour as searchers came and went. She'd left Lucy at home, thinking the dog would be too much of a distraction; now she wished she'd brought her along. She'd welcome anything to take her mind off of what was happening, if only for a second.

The parents of the boys and girls Emma had set out to meet arrived to take their children home. Patti from the Teocalli Tamale brought cold drinks and burritos for the searchers and Casey tried to eat, but she could only manage to choke down a few bites. Heather refused to eat or drink or even talk. She merely sat on the tailgate of someone's truck, which was doubling as both a bench and a desk, and stared at the map tacked there with blue painter's tape. The map showed the area around the trails, divided into numbered quadrants. As searchers returned from sweeping each quadrant, that area was highlighted with a yellow marker.

Many areas were highlighted now and still there was no sign of Emma.

By dusk both women were exhausted from the stress of waiting and hoping, but neither thought of leaving. Searchers donned headlamps and continued to go out, while others returned.

Max trudged down the trail a little after eight o'clock, Molly close behind him. They both walked with their heads down, shoulders hunched, the picture of exhaustion.

Heather stood as Max approached. "Hagan sent me to tell you we're going to have to shut down for the night soon," he said. "It's getting too dark and the country's rough. We don't want to end up having to rescue one of our own people."

Heather bit her lip and nodded but said nothing.

Max put his hand on her shoulder. "We've got the weather on our side. No rain in the forecast and the temps should only be in the upper forties."

Again Heather nodded. Casey wrapped her arms around herself and suppressed a shiver. Even in August the nights were cool at this elevation. Upper forties wasn't ordinarily life threatening, but if Emma had had the bad luck to fall into a stream or get wet, she could suffer from hypothermia.

So far Max had not looked at Casey. Now he glanced at her. "You okay?" he asked, his face too much in shadow for her to read his expression. It was a question he might have asked of anyone.

She nodded. "I'm worried."

"Yeah. We're all worried." He turned back to Heather. "Can I get you anything?"

She shook her head.

He slipped out of his pack. It landed on the ground with a heavy thud. Opening the top, he took out a sweatshirt, and a fleece jacket. "Take these. I don't need them."

They didn't protest, grateful for the warmth. Casey pulled the sweatshirt over her head and her breath caught as the familiar scent of Max surrounded her—coffee and chain oil, wintergreen Tic Tacs, wood smoke and an undefinable aroma that was simply…Max.

He started to turn away, but she put out a hand to stop him. "Thanks," she said. "For everything."

For one moment their eyes met, a look filled with regret and longing. She held her breath, waiting for him to say something—anything. To apologize. To suggest they try again.

But in the end he turned away without speaking.

He was halfway across the parking lot when the radio worn by the incident commander crackled. Everyone within hearing distance froze, listening.

"I've found her!" Ben's voice was loud in the night stillness. Jubilant. "She's okay. We're headed your way."

A cheer went up among the searchers. Heather fell against Casey, sobbing. Casey wrapped her arms around her friend and rocked her, tears flowing freely down her own cheeks. Max joined them, one hand on each of their shoulders. Casey was aware of little else besides that reassuring weight, the warmth of his skin seeping into her. Whatever was wrong between them, she could not stop loving him. If only she could convince him not to be afraid of that love and whatever it might bring.

The next hour was the slowest yet, waiting for Ben and Emma to appear. Casey stared toward the trailhead until her eyes stung and she had to force herself to blink. After twenty minutes, the radio crackled to life again. "We're getting there," Ben reassured them. "It's slow-going in the dark."

Hagan returned first and waited with the rest, silent, standing a little apart. Casey watched him. He never looked at Heather, merely waited calmly, hands clasped in front of his body. He was not aloof, but he had an air of reserve that all Heather's weeks and months of pursuing him had never succeeded in breeching.

If asked even a few days before, Casey would have told her friend to give up trying to change Hagan. For whatever reason, he had no desire to become involved with her. He was the way he was and she couldn't change him.

But now Casey felt she had no right to speak. Wasn't she just as bad, expecting Max to change his mind about marriage, to feel toward her what he'd apparently made up his mind—for whatever reason—to feel for no woman?

He left their side and went to stand beside Hagan. Two handsome men determined to avoid emotional entanglements. They valued independence over everything else. Even love.

"I see them!" someone said, and everyone's gaze strained down the trail. A single dot of light hovered in the air, small as a firefly at first, gradually growing larger. "It's Ben's headlamp," Heather said, walking toward the start of the trail.

Then she was running, stumbling over rocks and roots, Casey, Max and others close behind her. Ben and Emma ran, too, until mother and daughter met, crashing into each other's arms, tears flowing.

"I'm sorry," Emma sobbed. "I was stupid and angry and I never meant for this to happen."

"I know. I know," Heather crooned, stroking Emma's back and kissing her neck. "It's all right now. Everything's all right."

While Heather comforted her daughter, Ben related what had happened. "I found her in a little hollow back about a mile west of the lake," he said. "She was fast asleep. Worn out, I guess. I almost walked right past her, but something told me to stop and look closer."

"I did what you're supposed to do," Emma said, looking up at them. "All the books say if you get lost, to stay put. But I was beginning to think no one would ever come." She began crying again and Heather wept, too. Ben put his arms around them both and guided them back to the parking lot. "I'll take you home," he said softly. "Everything's going to be all right."

They left after exchanging hugs with most of the searchers who were there. As they drove away with Ben, the air of the crowd was jubilant. Men and women who had struggled on the edge of exhaustion only moments before were now full of energy, ready to party. Plans were made to meet at the Eldo and they parted to make their separate ways to town.

"Are you going to the Eldo?" Max asked Casey as she started back toward her vehicle.

She shook her head. "No. I need to go home and feed Lucy and take her out. Then I'm going to bed. I'm exhausted. What about you?"

"Molly and I are wiped. We're going to clean up and call it a night, too."

She waited for him to say something more, but he had nothing to add. It was a conversation he might have had with anyone—Trish or Patti or even Zephyr. Yet the air around them felt heavy with all the things they *hadn't* said. Things she didn't know how to begin to say.

"Well, see ya," he said, and turned away.

"Yeah. See ya." She'd see him every day. Always right across the hall or across the room or across the table. The man she most wanted to touch, always just out of reach.

Chapter Twelve

So what's your costume for the Arts and Film Festival Ball?"
Zephyr asked. A week after Emma's safe return, he and Max
leaned against the front counter at the coffee shop. As they
were closing up Mad Max's that afternoon they'd been re-
cruited as taste testers for the smoothies Trish had added to
the coffee shop's menu.

"I don't know that I'm going to the ball this year," Max
said.

Trish and Zephyr stared at him. "You haven't missed a
party like this since you moved to C.B.," Trish said.

"I'm going as one of the king's men," Zephyr said.

"All the king's horses and all the king's men…" Trish
shook her head. "You ought to go as one of the horses. The
back half."

He stuck his tongue out at her. It was blue, from his blue-
berry-banana smoothie.

Max ignored them. He didn't feel much like partying these
days. Being around a bunch of other people having fun only
made him feel more out of sorts. Maybe he needed a change
of scenery. A view that didn't include a certain beautiful
blonde who lived across the hall.

"How's your smoothie?" Trish asked. "Too much papaya?"

"Huh?" He looked at her, then into the tall paper cup in front of him. "Yeah, it's good."

"Yeah, too much papaya or not?"

He took a sip. "I don't know a papaya from a pineapple, so you'd better ask somebody else."

"Dude, you are a serious downer these days, you know that?" Zephyr said.

Max scowled. "Who asked you?"

"Why don't you just admit you're upset because you blew it with Casey?" Trish said. "Patch things up with her and we'll all feel better."

"What do you mean *I* blew it?" He stood straighter. "Is that what she's been saying?"

"She hasn't said anything," Trish said. "She has too much class for that. Though I know she's as broken up about this as you are."

His chest tightened at the idea that Casey was hurting because of him. She'd looked okay every time he'd seen her. Not much different than she'd always looked—beautiful. Sexy. Sweet. He'd alternated between being happy that she was taking their breakup so well and being depressed that he hadn't meant more to her. But maybe it was only that she did a better job of hiding her feelings than he did. "Why do you automatically assume I'm the one who screwed up?" he asked.

She rested her elbows on the counter and leaned toward him. "Face it, Max, you have a rep. Things get serious with a woman and you run the other way." She shook her head. "I really thought you'd be different with Casey."

"I didn't run away," he said. Not really. It wasn't running to leave a hopeless situation. He and Casey would never see eye to eye on the whole marriage thing. And no matter what she said about not wanting to rush into anything, he'd always know she had that dress hanging in her closet, waiting for wedding bells to ring.

"You're a blockhead," Zephyr said.

He turned to face the musician. "What do you know about it?" he asked. "Have you ever even have a steady girlfriend?"

"Rock musicians don't have steady girls," Zephyr said. "We have groupies."

"So what do you know about love?" Trish asked Zephyr.

He looked offended. "Duh? Musicians know about love. Why do you think we write so many songs about it?"

"Who said anything about love?" Max asked. He'd admitted his feelings to Casey, but now he wished he never had. It made it that much harder to pretend there hadn't been something special between them.

The evening when Emma was found, when he'd looked into Casey's eyes there at the trailhead parking lot, he'd seen all her love shining out at him, as fresh and deep as when they'd lain together in each other's arms. It had been all he could do then not to pull her into his arms, but he'd known doing so would only lead to them both being hurt all over again. It probably didn't make sense to her—hell, it didn't always make sense to him—but whatever it took to be good at all the ordinary grown-up things in life—college, careers, marriage—he didn't have that in him. He'd messed up every time he'd tried one of them. Casey didn't want to believe that of him, but it was true and he was determined not to hurt them both any more than he already had.

Trish gave him a pitying look. "All anyone had to do was look at the two of you together to know you had the real thing going on," she said.

"Yeah, you two were made for each other." Zephyr sucked up the last of his smoothie, making loud slurping noises. He handed his empty cup to Trish. "Let me try one of those papaya things."

She shook her head, but took the cup and turned to her blender.

"If you don't go to the ball, who's going to be the Mad Hatter?" Zephyr asked. "You're a natural for the role. No one else would dare take it."

"What's Casey coming as?" Max asked Trish, raising his voice to be heard over the whir of the blender.

She shrugged. "I don't know."

She poured the contents of the blender into a cup and handed it to Zephyr. "You really should go to the ball," she said to Max. "If you don't everyone will talk."

"Yeah, and you know Casey will be there," Zephyr said. "She has to go because of her job with the chamber."

"Then that's one more reason I shouldn't go," Max said.

"Uh-uh," Trish said. "Then everyone might think you hate each other."

"I don't hate her. I still like her." He still loved her, but there was nothing he could do about that.

"Then if you're not there, they'll think you're feeling guilty," Trish said. "That maybe you did something *really* terrible to her."

He frowned at her. "They won't think that unless you two start some kind of rumor."

Zephyr grinned and turned to Trish. "We could do that, couldn't we?"

"Absolutely. Rumors are us." She folded her arms and studied Max. "Do you have any preference as to the terrible thing you supposedly did?"

"Some friends you two are."

"So you'll be at the ball?" Trish asked.

"I have a feeling if I didn't show up, you two would come drag me out of my apartment and *force* me to go."

She looked him up and down. "We might have to bring along some help, but that could be arranged."

She was probably just teasing. But maybe not. People around here took the attitude they knew what was best for their friends.

Sometimes they were even right.

CASEY SUSPECTED something was up when Ben began showing up to take Heather to lunch. Every day.

The chamber director had taken to humming as she worked, a satisfied half smile on her face that Casey suspected had nothing to do with the upcoming Arts and Film Festival.

When Hagan stopped by with information about a silent auction to benefit Search and Rescue, Heather hadn't even cut short her phone conversation with a tourist in order to speak with him. But when Casey asked if there was anything Heather wanted to talk about, her coworker had merely smiled and made some vague reply about turning over a new leaf.

Emma was different these days, too. Whether shaken by her close call on the hiking trail or by her mother's tears, the girl had grown up a great deal in a very short time. On Ben's advice, Heather had asked Emma to choose her own punishment for her disobedience and lying. They'd settled on being grounded for a month and the donation of a month's allowance to the Search and Rescue group—tougher punishment than Heather herself might have meted out.

Though fall was still a month away, the cooler nights hinted at the changing seasons and everywhere Casey looked, things felt different.

For one thing, Paul's letters had stopped.

They'd been coming for so long now that the first week one didn't arrived, she'd dismissed it as a glitch in the postal system. When the second week passed with no letter, she'd felt an odd sensation. Not relief exactly, merely as if something had shifted. Odd as it seemed, those letters had been a kind of tie to her old life. Now that tie was gone and she felt adrift. No Paul.

No Max.

One man she could do without, but the other she still longed for. So much for making it on her own. It was lonely out here by herself, though she hoped with time that feeling would lessen. After all, she had plenty of friends, work she enjoyed and a whole fall and winter of new activities, festivals and celebrations to look forward to.

Including the Arts and Film Festival Ball. Heather pressed her to decide on a costume. "If you wait too long, all the good characters will be gone," she said. "You'll have to be an anonymous playing card or something."

"It's been a long time since I've read *Alice's Adventures in Wonderland*," Casey said. "I don't remember all the characters."

"There's the Mad Hatter and the Red Queen. Alice, of course. Tweedledee and Tweedledum. The Cheshire Cat. The Dormouse. Ben's going as the March Hare." She smiled, though why the thought of the doctor in a rabbit costume should make her smile, Casey couldn't imagine.

"What are you going as?" she asked.

"I'm going as the White Queen. I have the perfect costume." She grinned. "You should go as the Red Queen. I'm sure no one else is doing it. Or if they are, they won't be as perfect at it as you would."

"I wore red to the Flauschink Polka Ball."

"You look good in red. It can be your signature," Heather said. "You can specialize in red costumes. It will make it easy to put together your costume closet."

"My costume closet?"

"After you've been here a while, you can't help but end up with a whole bunch of different costumes." Heather shrugged. "Is it any wonder Halloween is my favorite holiday?"

Their conversation was cut short by a ringing phone. Casey spent the next hour fielding questions from potential visitors and artists who wanted to submit work to the festival. She was explaining the application procedure to a painter from Denver when Ben walked in. He waved to her, then headed for Heather's desk.

Casey hung up in time to hear him say, "I won't be able to go to lunch with you today. I have to be in Gunnison to assist with a hip replacement for one of my patients."

"That's all right," Heather said. "I'll go home and eat with Emma."

"Tell her I said hello."

"I'll do that."

They grinned at each other. Casey had the sudden impression that if she hadn't been there, they would have kissed.

As soon as Ben was out the door, she turned to Heather. "What is going on?" she asked.

"What do you mean?" Heather shuffled papers and refused to meet Casey's eyes.

"I mean, what is going on between you and Ben? You two have been spending a lot of time together and you definitely don't look at each other the way casual friends look at each other." Come to think of it, she'd never seen Heather look at any man that way—not even Hagan.

Heather dropped into a chair, her face practically glowing. "I think I'm in love," she said.

"With Ben?"

She nodded.

Casey swiveled her chair to face her friend. "When did this happen?" she asked.

Heather shrugged. "It just…happened."

"But recently." Casey tried to think when she'd first noticed the change in Heather. "Since Emma's rescue?"

"Yes…." Heather twisted her hands together in her lap. "The whole time I was waiting for word of Emma, I was feeling so guilty, thinking I should have done something to save her from herself."

"You did what you could. You couldn't predict she'd run off the way she did."

"I still felt guilty." Heather glanced at her. "You'll understand one day—it's a mom thing. Anyway, I was really beating up on myself. If only I'd remarried after her father and I divorced. If only I'd focused more on her and less on Hagan. If only, if only…" She shook her head. "Then when I saw her coming up the trail with Ben and she told me how great he'd been, how much she liked him, it just hit me. Ben is the kind of man Emma and I both need in our lives. He's smart, warm, funny, dependable…."

"Not as handsome or sexy as Hagan," Casey pointed out.

"I didn't think so at first, but now…" She blushed to the roots of her hair. "Now I know he really *is* sexy."

Casey laughed. It was a kick to see Heather so happy. "Does he feel the same way?"

"Yes! That first night, after he took us home and Emma was in bed, he and I stayed up talking—about everything. He told me how he'd ended up out here after his first marriage ended—I told him about my divorce. I even told him about Hagan."

"Get out! What did he say?"

"He told me Hagan has women following him everywhere, but none of them mean anything to him. He thinks Hagan won't ever be serious about a woman until he meets one who doesn't fall all over herself over him."

"Don't let that secret out of the bag," Casey said. "He'll be surrounded by women pretending to play hard to get."

Heather laughed. "I'd been fantasizing about Hagan for so long that when I was with a real man—with Ben—it was something of a shock. I'd forgotten what it was like not to have to work so hard to get a guy's attention. And what it was like to have a real conversation."

"I'm happy for you," Casey said. "That's terrific."

Heather's expression sobered. "I wish things had worked out better for you and Max. I really thought you would be the woman to change him."

Casey had thought so, too—Max had seen that before she did. No matter how much she assured him she valued his friendship, deep inside she knew she really wanted more. It was probably why she'd agreed to marry Paul even though she didn't love him. "You couldn't change Hagan," she said.

"No...but Ben managed to change me." Her chair squeaked as she shifted in it. "He didn't really change *me,* but he changed my mind about the kind of man I wanted."

"I don't think Max is going to change."

"Has he said anything to you about what happened?" Heather asked.

Casey shook her head. "No. I mean, I see him sometimes in the hallway outside my apartment, or at the Eldo or in the coffee shop or other places around town."

"It's almost impossible not to run into people over and over again in a town this small," Heather said.

Casey nodded. "We're always polite. I mean, we don't hate each other or anything."

"It would probably be easier if you did."

"I could never hate Max." In spite of everything, she still thought of him as a good friend. "I just wish I understood him better."

"He's probably saying the same thing about you," Heather said.

The outer door to the chamber offices opened and they broke off their conversation. Casey carried a stack of folders to the back, while Heather turned to greet the new arrival.

After she and Heather returned from lunch, Casey devoted herself to catching up on the mountain of paperwork that needed to be filed. She could have left the job for Margie, but she enjoyed hiding out in the back room, letting her mind wander as she alphabetized folders and sorted papers. She was thumbing through folders in a tall filing cabinet when Heather called to her. "Casey, there's someone here to see you!"

Me? Who would show up to see her? She set the unfiled papers on top of the cabinet and started toward the front room.

She almost collided with Heather in the doorway. "Why didn't you tell me he was so good-looking?" Heather asked, her eyes bright with excitement.

"Tell you *who* was good-looking?" Casey stared at her friend, confused. "Who's out there?"

"I don't want to spoil the surprise." Heather nudged her toward the front. "Go on. Don't keep him waiting."

The man's back was to her as he studied the brochure rack. Something about the set of his shoulders, his navy blazer and his khaki trousers, so different from the blue jeans and Dockers favored by local men, made Casey freeze. She shut her eyes and took in a deep breath. Obviously, she was under more stress than she thought. There was no reason that what her mind seemed to be telling her should be true.

She must have made a noise of some kind. The man turned around and smiled at her. "Hello, Casey," he said.

"Wh-what are you doing here?" She forced herself to walk toward him on stiff legs.

"I came to take you home. Where you belong."

Heather appeared and nudged Casey in the side. "Aren't you going to introduce me to your friend?" she asked.

Casey cleared her throat. "Sure. Um, Heather Allison, this is Paul. Paul Rittinghouse."

Chapter Thirteen

Heather shook Paul's hand, then made a show of checking her watch. "I can't believe it's after three already. Casey, if you want to take off early, you can. I know you and Paul have a lot of catching up to do."

Casey stared at Heather, but her friend either wasn't getting it or was deliberately ignoring all the signals she was sending. She didn't want to go anywhere with Paul. She didn't want to see Paul. She didn't have anything to say to him. "Thanks, but I really have a lot to do," she said. She glanced at Paul. "I might even have to work late."

"Don't be ridiculous," Heather said. "Anything you have to do will still be waiting for you tomorrow."

"I really don't want to take off early," she said, staring at Heather.

"Oh. Okay." Heather glanced at Paul.

"Why don't I come back at six?" he said. "Casey and I can have dinner together and catch up." He smiled at both women, then left before Casey could object.

When he was gone Casey leaned against the desk and waited for her heartbeat to slow. "He stopped writing, so I thought he'd finally given up," she said.

"He's obviously crazy about you," Heather said. "I think it's sweet."

"I think it's creepy." She pushed herself away from the desk and headed for the back room. "And I don't want to talk about it."

But she had plenty of time to think as she sorted and alphabetized and stuffed paperwork into folders. Why was Paul here? Did he really think he could talk her into going back to Chicago with him? Did he love her that much?

The idea made a knot of pain in the middle of her stomach. She didn't want Paul to love her. Believing that would make it too easy to feel sorry for him and add to her guilt at leaving him.

Heather obviously thought she was crazy to have ditched a man like Paul—especially if she was turning her back on him for a man who had made it clear they had no future together. It was as if the tables had turned and now she was the one moping over the wrong man. Was Paul like Ben—the quiet good guy, waiting on the sidelines for his opportunity?

She shoved a fat sheaf of telephone logs into an already-overstuffed folder and slammed shut the filing-cabinet door. It was all such a mess. *She* was a mess.

When she thought of Max, she saw a man with a distorted view of himself. What if she was suffering from the same problem? She was sure she wasn't cut out to be a society woman and political wife, but what if that was exactly what she was meant to be? It was certainly what she'd been raised to be. What if she'd run away from the perfect life for her out of childish stubbornness?

At precisely six o'clock, Paul returned to the chamber offices. He was dressed more casually now, in designer jeans and a pale peach cotton shirt with a banded collar. His hair was windblown, the tips lightened by the sun—or an artful hairdresser. He had the kind of smile that probably made most women weak at the knees but when he turned it on her she felt…nothing.

"Ready for dinner?" he asked.

"I have to take Lucy home and look after her." She snapped the dog's leash to her collar, avoiding Paul's eyes.

"You have a dog?" From his tone of voice, he might as well have been asking if she had suddenly grown a large, hairy wart.

"Yes, I have a dog."

"I'll look after Lucy." Heather took the leash from Casey's hand. "You two have a good time and don't worry about a thing."

Casey frowned, but let Heather take Lucy. At least this way she'd avoid having Paul follow her to her apartment.

"You two have a wonderful time," Heather said as she gathered her own belongings and prepared to lock up for the night. She didn't say she expected a full report in the morning, but Casey knew she would.

Paul stopped on the sidewalk outside the chamber building and slipped on a pair of sunglasses. "What is there to eat in this place?" he asked.

"What are you hungry for?"

"I could go for some sushi."

Of course. She hated sushi. And she couldn't help but think he'd deliberately chosen food he was sure this small Western town wouldn't be able to provide. "We have sushi." She started down the sidewalk. "Lobar is supposed to have great sushi."

He grabbed her arm and pulled her back. "On second thought, I don't trust sushi out here in the back of beyond. They probably use leftover bait or something."

At one time she would have ignored the remark, not wanting to make a scene or start a fight. Now she turned to face him. "Stop it right now or I won't go to dinner with you."

"Stop what?" He dipped his head and looked at her over the top of his sunglasses.

"Stop making your snobby, insulting remarks. This town is my home now. I like it here and these people are my friends."

To her surprise, he looked contrite. "You're right," he said. "I apologize. I'm on edge because I'm nervous. And maybe I'm trying to impress you."

The confession caught her off guard. "You don't have to impress me," she said.

"I don't care where we eat." He looked around at the brightly colored buildings along Elk Avenue. "You choose."

She decided on the Wooden Nickel. It was big enough, with enough dim corners, that with luck she wouldn't run into anyone she knew.

As if that were really possible. The hostess who seated them was a good friend of Heather's and their waitress, Steffie, had helped Casey hand out refreshments at the bike race. Steffie subtly checked out Paul and gave Casey a thumbs-up sign behind his back.

Casey ignored the gesture and slid into a booth across from him. "They have good burgers here," she said, picking up a menu.

"You look great," Paul said. "How have you been?"

"I've been good. I'm happy here. And I have no intention of moving back to Chicago."

He ignored her protest and studied the menu. "I think I feel like a steak. And maybe some wine."

She waited for him to disparage the wine list, but true to his earlier promise, he held his tongue. When Steffie returned to take their orders he was charming, even flirtatious. She sent Casey another look, this one envious. If Paul would forget about her, he could have half the women in town after him by tomorrow morning.

He kept the conversation casual through their salads and entrées, discussing friends they had in common, her father's mayoral campaign and his own law practice. He didn't ask what she'd been doing since she left Chicago and she didn't volunteer any information. Her life here in Crested Butte was something that belonged only to her; she wasn't inclined to share it with him in even a small way.

By the time their cheesecake and coffee arrived, she could contain herself no longer. "Paul, what are you doing here?" she asked. "Why did you keep writing me when I never answered your letters?"

He set aside his fork and wiped his mouth with his napkin, then fixed her with a gaze that must have proven useful in impressing prospective clients. "I'll do whatever it takes to convince you you've made a huge mistake." He reached across the table and took her hand. "You and I are prefect for one another. Everyone says so."

She pulled her hand away. "Paul, I am not perfect for you. How could you think that after I left you at the altar? I walked out on our wedding day."

He looked pained. "You panicked," he said. "You got cold feet. I understand—"

"I don't love you."

He fell silent and stared at her a long moment. The scrape of cutlery on china, the low murmur of voices and occasional bursts of laughter from others around them, even the music from the speakers on the ceiling faded, swallowed up by that deadly silence. Casey looked at her plate and debated getting up and leaving now, while she still clung to some shred of dignity.

"You're confusing love with some crazy, earthshaking infatuation," Paul said finally. "That isn't love. That's... hormones."

His dismissive tone angered her. She raised her head to look at him. "Hormones—physical attraction—are an important part of love," she said.

"You never seemed to have any problem with the physical aspect of our relationship when we were dating," he said.

She felt her cheeks warm. Sex with Paul had been... adequate. Not bad, but not great. They'd been physically compatible but some emotional element had been missing. She had told herself that was the way things were supposed to be—that the intense closeness and passion portrayed in movies and books and music were merely fantasies, never meant to be real.

Now she looked across the table at him and felt...nothing. Not the least little zing of attraction. It was as if she were having dinner with a male cousin—or someone she'd hired to do her taxes.

"Honestly, you're too young to be having a midlife crisis," he said.

Now her face was positively burning, but not from embarrassment. "Is that what you think this is?" she asked. "Some phase I'm going through?"

"Crisis, a phase, insanity—call it anything you like. Whatever's gotten into you, I'm certain it's temporary. As soon as you come to your senses you'll realize I'm right." He smiled. "You'll thank me one day for saving you from yourself."

"I do not need saving." If the waitress hadn't already cleared away their glasses of ice water, Casey would have been tempted to empty one into his lap. The man obviously needed something to snap him back to reality. "And I'm not crazy. In fact, you're the one who's delusional. You refuse to accept that I have come to my senses." She stood and picked up her purse. "I don't love you," she said. "I won't marry you. I won't go back to Chicago with you." She had the sense that everyone around them was watching and listening, not even attempting subtlety. Tomorrow half a dozen versions of this conversation would be repeated around town.

"What are you going to do?" Paul asked. His voice turned nasty. "Stay here? In this…this rural tourist trap? Mooning over some muscle-bound ski bum?"

She winced. Obviously someone had filled Paul in on her late lamented romance with Max. Anyone he met at a coffee shop or bar this afternoon might have offered the details if probed carefully. Being a lawyer, Paul was an expert at careful probing.

"Crested Butte is not a tourist trap," she said. *And Max is not a ski bum. And I'm not mooning over him. Not much, anyway.* "I'm living the life I want here. It's not always perfect and some days I have to make things up as I go along. There's no script written by you or my mother or anyone else that I have to follow. But that's okay. I'm making my own decisions, figuring out what I want to do."

Paul shook his head. "You're making a big mistake."

"If I am, then that's part of it. At least now when things go wrong, I know I'm the only one responsible."

His eyes met hers. No matter what Heather thought about his devotion to her, Casey saw no love in those brown depths—only the anger of a spoiled man who hasn't gotten his way. "Do you really want to waste your life this way— working a dead-end job, living in a cheap apartment, dressing like an extra in some off-off-Broadway production of *Annie Get Your Gun?*"

She sighed. "Go home, Paul. You don't belong here."

"Neither do you." He slid out of the booth to stand in front of her. "This is your last chance," he said. "Come home with me. In a few weeks everyone will forgive you and this will all seem like a bad dream."

"This is like a dream. A good one." She opened her purse and took out two twenties and laid them on the table. "That's for my half of dinner. Goodbye."

She turned and hurried away, running once she was out the door, half afraid he'd pursue her.

She didn't stop until she reached her apartment.

As she fumbled for her key, gasping for breath, she looked across the hall to Max's closed door. She wished she had the courage to knock and ask to be let in. To cry on his shoulder and feel his strong arms around her.

She settled instead for letting Lucy comfort her. The puppy curled on the bed beside her and licked at her tears. "Be glad you don't have to deal with men yet," she told the dog. "I don't know which are worse, the ones you love or the ones you don't."

BRYAN SHOWED UP at Max's shop the next morning. "Hey, Max, can I talk to you for a minute?" he asked.

"Sure." Max looked up from the chain ring he was cleaning. "What's up?"

"You know I've been dating Steffie Watson?" Bryan slid onto a stool beside Max's workbench. "She's a waitress over at the Wooden Nickel. Well, she's really an accountant, but she does the waitressing to earn extra money."

Max nodded. He'd dated Steffie at one time, too, though he saw no reason to point this out to Bryan. Anyway, they'd only gone out a few times. They didn't really click. "How's that working for you?" he asked.

"Good. We have a lot of fun together."

"That's good." He sprayed more cleaner on the chain ring and scrubbed it with a brush. "So, is that all you wanted to tell me?"

"No." Bryan shoved his hands in his back pocket. "Steffie worked last night," he said. "She said Casey came in with some guy."

"Oh?" His hand slipped and he gashed his finger on the sharp teeth of the chain ring, but he scarcely felt it. He sucked on the injury, his thoughts whirling. Realistically, he'd known Casey would eventually date other men. She was too great a gal—pretty, sweet, fun—to stay single long. But he thought he'd have a little more time to get used to the idea first. "Who was it?" he asked.

Bryan shook his head. "Steffie didn't know." He coughed. "But she said he was good-looking. And he wore expensive clothes."

"A tourist?" His stomach tightened.

Bryan shrugged. "Maybe."

Max could picture it—some guy walks into the chamber to ask directions. He and Casey get to talking and the next thing anybody knows, they're having dinner together. "And you're telling me this why?" he asked.

"I just thought you'd want to know."

"Why would I want to know?" He attacked the chain ring with fresh vigor, as if the grease and grime embedded there were all the ugly thoughts currently racing through his mind.

"I don't know. I guess…in case you wanted to do something about it."

"Casey and I split up. There's nothing I could do about it."

"Okay. Well…" Bryan slid off the stood and backed toward the door. "I just thought you'd like to know, that's all."

On his way out the door, Bryan almost collided with Zephyr. "I just heard Casey's old boyfriend is back in town," Zephyr announced.

Bryan and Max both stared at him. "Is that who she was having dinner with last night?" Bryan asked.

"I guess so." Zephyr hopped onto a stool behind the front counter.

"Paul is here?" Max asked. "In Crested Butte?"

"Is that his name?" Zephyr asked. "Tall guy, expensive haircut, clothes that all match?"

"I don't know what he looks like," Max said. "How do you know her boyfriend is here?"

"You know Graciela Morgan?" Zephyr asked. "She dates the bass player in my band and works as a maid over at the Christiana Guesthaus. She overheard this guy talking on the phone and put two and two together."

"Does Graciela always eavesdrop on the hotel guests?" Max asked.

"I don't think so, but she said this guy was really hot, so she was checking him out." Zephyr shrugged, as if this explained everything.

Why did everyone feel compelled to point out how *hot* the guy was? "I heard he's a real jerk," he said.

"Steffie said he was really charming." Bryan frowned. "She never calls me charming."

"Graciela says he tips good," Zephyr offered.

Max gave up and tossed aside the brush. "What do you expect me to do about it?" he snapped.

"Maybe you should challenge him to a fight," Zephyr said. He rubbed his hands together. "Like a duel. The winner gets the girl."

"That's crazy," Max said.

"No, it'd be great," Zephyr said. "You're bigger than he is, so you'd be sure to win."

"Yeah, if he's some rich guy from the city, he's probably not all that tough," Bryan said.

"Shut up, both of you. I'm not going to fight anybody." Not that the thought of showing up this guy didn't tempt him. "If Casey wants to see him, it's none of my business." He glanced at Bryan. "Did Steffie say anything about how Casey acted at the dinner? Was she having a good time?"

Bryan shrugged. "She didn't say. I mean, they weren't making out at the table or anything, but she didn't dump her drink on him or throw food, either."

"Do people really do that?" Zephyr asked. "Throw food?"

"Steffie says she's seen all kinds of weird stuff. There was this couple one time who—"

"If you don't mind," Max inserted himself between them. "I've got work to do. And so does Zephyr."

"Sure." Bryan started toward the door. "I just thought you'd want to know."

When Bryan was gone, Zephyr looked at Max. "What are you going to do about Casey and this guy?" he asked.

"I'm not going to do anything," Max said.

"Aww, man, that's not how it's supposed to work!"

Max frowned at him. "What do you mean? How what's supposed to work?"

Zephyr slid off the stool. "When the old boyfriend of the woman you love shows up, you're supposed to realize how much she means to you and rush to her and declare your undying love."

Max stared at him. "Where do you get this stuff?"

"Books. Movies. Music. It's everywhere. Haven't you been paying attention?"

Max put his hand on Zephyr's shoulder. "I know this is hard for you to grasp, but the real world doesn't always work like books and movies—or even music," he said. "Casey and I aren't a couple anymore. It didn't work out for us. We want different things in life."

"Yeah, yeah, yeah." Zephyr waved away Max's logic. "She wants the ring and the preacher and all of that and you just want to keep going on like you always have. Except you can't be like you always were anymore, because you went and fell in love with her and love changes everything. There's a song that says that, you know."

Max blinked. He must be in trouble now, because Zephyr was starting to make sense. He took his hand away and stepped back behind the counter. "If Casey wants to go back to Chicago with her rich, good-looking jerk of a boyfriend, then maybe that's exactly where she belongs. I don't have the right to stop her."

"If you don't try, you'll never know what she really wants, will you?"

Max frowned. "If she goes with him, it will be because she wants to."

"Now who's living in fantasyland?" Zephyr snorted. "I'm gonna write a song about you, dude. I'm gonna call it 'He Got His Way and Lost Everything Else.'"

"Shut up and go unpack the order that came in yesterday."

Humming to himself, Zephyr shuffled off to the storeroom. Max tried to focus on cleaning and reinstalling the chain ring, but his thoughts continually veered back to Casey. What did she see in a guy like Paul? Other than looks and money—and the fact that he'd written her every week for months and finally followed her all the way from Chicago. Women didn't want that kind of smothering devotion, did they?

Besides, Casey loved *him!* She'd said so and she wasn't the type to lie. The two of them understood each other. They connected on a level that went beyond the physical.

Casey didn't care about status and money and other people's expectations. She'd left Chicago to get away from all that, the way he'd left Connecticut. She liked dogs and being outdoors and hanging out with friends—the things he liked.

When he was with her, he never felt like a failure. In fact, with Casey he'd felt as if he had something everyone else should be jealous of.

So why didn't you bother to tell her any of this, you idiot?

Maybe because he'd gotten so used to thinking certain things were out of his reach he hadn't really considered any other possibility. A man who never liked complications, he'd taken the easy way out: he'd decided years ago he wasn't the marrying kind and had lived that way ever since. No messy emotions, no agonizing over the future. He'd keep his personal life simple, the way he did everything else.

He'd set himself up to never have to fail at anything important and almost made the biggest mistake of all—believing that refusing to change made him smart when it really only made him stubborn.

"Brains had nothing to do with it," he mumbled.

So what was he going to do now? He glanced toward the back room, tempted to ask Zephyr if he had any more rock-star advice. But he discarded the idea. He'd gotten himself into this mess. Now he had to figure it out. He only hoped he wasn't too late.

"I HEARD YOUR OLD FLAME left town last night," Heather said as she and Casey opened the chamber offices Friday morning.

"I guess so." Casey tossed her purse onto her desk.

"You two had a big blowup at the Wooden Nickel," Heather said.

"Does the whole town know every detail of my personal life?" Casey snapped.

"Probably." Heather put her arm around Casey's shoulders. "It's only because we're your friends and we care about you. If Paul had done anything out of line, you can bet half a dozen people would have stepped up to straighten him out."

She couldn't help but smile at that idea. It was nice, really, having so many people watching her back. People she knew she could count on if she needed help or support.

"So he really wasn't The One," Heather said, settling at her desk.

"He was never The One."

"And Max is."

She looked sharply at her friend. "No, Max is not The One, either. He's not interested in a home and family and all the things I really do want—someday." Although Max *could* have been The One. Every time she allowed her mind to drift to fantasies of herself wearing her wedding gown or holding a baby it was always Max there beside her.

"You could always play around with Max until the right guy does come along," Heather said.

"And how is this man supposed to know I'm available if I'm dating another man?" Not that it wasn't tempting to go back to the way things were—she and Max in love, having fun, going for bike rides and hikes, talking the way they could always talk about anything. They could probably go on that way for years. But the knowledge that it wasn't really permanent would always hang between them.

The sound of the door opening signaled it was time to get

to work. Casey was glad for the opportunity to drop the subject of her love life—or lack thereof—until she looked up and found a grinning Jerry Rydell standing in front of her desk. "Hello, Jerry," she said. "What can I do for you this morning?"

Grin fixed firmly in place, he shuffled nervously, reminding her too much of the first time they'd met, when he'd welcomed her to Crested Butte with his gift of moose poop. "I was wondering if you'd be my date for the Arts and Film Festival Ball," he asked.

She blinked. "I—I'm flattered, Jerry, but I wasn't planning on going with a date. I…well, I'm sort of working that night, you know. As a representative of the chamber and all."

Heather didn't even pretend not to be eavesdropping. "There's no reason you can't take a date," she said.

"I'm going as the Cheshire Cat," Jerry volunteered.

Maybe that explained the grin. "Thanks, but I prefer to go alone."

He shrugged. "Thought it was worth a try, since you're not dating Max anymore and I heard you ran that Chicago guy out of town." He lifted his hand in a salute. "I'll see you two ladies tonight."

When he was gone, Casey turned to Heather. "You didn't have anything to do with that, did you?"

"Anything to do with what?" She shuffled papers, looking anything but innocent.

"Heather, please, please, *please* do not try to set me up. When I'm ready to date, I'll find my own man."

"I wasn't trying to set you up," Heather protested. "I saw Jerry in the coffee shop this morning and suggested he stop by, is all."

"Well, don't do it again."

"I hope you're not going to waste your time pining for Max, when you could be finding a man who'll treat you the way you deserve to be treated."

Casey stared at Heather. "You're one to talk," she said. "How many months did you moon after Hagan? You wouldn't listen to anyone who told you it was hopeless."

"Exactly. I learned from my mistake and I'd hate to see you make the same one."

Casey turned back to her desk, struggling to keep her expression calm. "I'm not pining. But I see no point in rushing into anything," she said. "Besides, I really do prefer to go to the ball by myself. I think it'll be more fun that way."

And if Max was at the ball, she didn't want another man to keep her from talking to him. She had a few things she needed to say to him—things he needed to hear before she gave up on him for good.

Chapter Fourteen

Max adjusted his bow tie and studied his reflection in the bathroom mirror. The stiff white-collared shirt, striped vest and trousers, red tailcoat and oversize top hat completed his costume as the Mad Hatter. There'd been no question this would be his costume. He was Mad Max, after all. The original wild man of Crested Butte.

Except he didn't feel all that wild lately. He couldn't remember the last time he'd partied until dawn or done something truly outrageous—such as the time he, Zephyr and Bryan had streaked down Elk Avenue as an unscheduled finale to the Fourth of July parade. Was age catching up with him or had something else about him changed?

He turned from the mirror and went into the bedroom. "Come on, Molly," he called. "I'll take you out before I head to the party."

The dog wagged her tail, but didn't move from her bed in the corner.

"What is it, girl?" he asked, going over to her. "Is something wrong?"

He was about to kneel beside her when a pounding on his door startled him. "Max! Max, are you home?"

He was at the door in a few steps and pulled it open to find a mud-streaked man leaning against the wall. "Sorry to bother you," the man, Gary Prentice, said. "But I need a new wheel right away." He held up a seriously bent bike wheel. "Would you mind checking to see if you have one in stock?"

"What did you do?" Max asked.

Gary made a face. "I was coming down a trail too fast, hit a rock and crashed and burned." He examined a still-bleeding scratch on his elbow. "I was just banged up a little, but my bike bought it." He looked at Max again. "I wouldn't bother you unless it was an emergency. Me and my brother are leaving on a week-long ride tomorrow morning. I won't be able to go if I can't get my bike fixed."

"Ok. Hang on a minute, I'll get my key."

Five minutes later, he and Gary were in the storeroom, digging through a stack of wheels. "I think this is the right one." Max held up a new wheel.

Gary checked it against the bent one in his hand. "Looks like it'll work."

"You need help putting it on?" Max asked.

"Nah, I can do it. How much do I owe you?"

Max rang up the purchase and accepted Gary's credit card.

"Thanks," Gary said as he signed the card slip. "You really saved my life here."

"Sure." Max walked with him to the door. "Good luck with your trip."

"Thanks. Have fun at your party."

"Right." It was going to be a barrel of laughs. A hundred zany characters and one Mad Hatter who wasn't so mad anymore—and a Red Queen who had either ruined his life or done him a huge favor. The verdict wasn't in on that one yet.

Back upstairs, he called Molly again. "Come on, girl. Time to go out."

The dog didn't respond to his call.

He found her in the bedroom on her bed. "Molly?" She raised her head and looked at him forlornly. He knelt beside her. "Molly? What is it, girl?"

She put her head down and sighed—an unhappy sound.

He stood and patted his thighs. "Come on, girl. You need to go out."

She struggled to her feet, walked stiffly toward him, hobbling on three legs before collapsing once more to the rug at his feet.

Alarmed, he ran to the phone and punched in the number for his vet. "Hello. Our offices are closed at the moment. For emergency service, please call Gunnison Animal Hospital—" He slammed down the phone. Gunnison was a half hour away, then he'd have to wait at the clinic there. By the time he got back the ball would be over. Worse, it would mean making Molly wait all that time for treatment.

He picked up the phone again and punched in another number.

"Hello?" Ben's voice answered.

"Ben, can you meet me over at your clinic? It's an emergency."

"Max, what happened? Are you hurt?"

"Not me. It's Molly. Something's wrong with her. She's lame in one leg and she looks like she feels terrible."

"Molly? Max, I'm a doctor, not a veterinarian."

"I know, but the vet is closed. You can at least examine her and let me know if I need to take her to Gunnison."

Ben sighed. "All right, I'll meet you at the clinic. But hurry. I don't want to be late for the ball."

CASEY HAD TO ADMIT SHE WAS PLEASED with her Red Queen costume. She and Heather had reworked a red taffeta gown from the thrift store, adding a net train and an Elizabethan-style ruff and appliquéing large sequined hearts to the skirt. A dime-store tiara completed the costume. When she arrived at the Center for the Arts, she received many compliments from the women and more than one appreciative second look from the men in attendance.

Now she stood with Heather just inside the door, welcoming the other guests and providing directions to food and drink. After an initial rush of arrivals the traffic had slowed to a trickle. Heather frowned at the filling room. "Where is Ben?" she fretted. "He should have been here by now."

"He'll be here," Casey reassured her. "Ben's very dependable."

"You're right," Heather said. "I don't know why I worry." She smiled. "I think we can relinquish our door duties now and enjoy ourselves. Trish said something about saving seats for us at her table."

"They're in the back corner," Casey said, nodding toward a group of tables far from the dance floor.

Two tables had been pushed together to accommodate the group, which consisted of Bryan and Steffie dressed as Tweedledee and Tweedledum, Trish as the Dormouse—complete with a nightcap and pillow—Patti as Alice, Hagan, carrying a hookah, as the Caterpillar and Zephyr, who was wearing a white dinner jacket, black checked pants, sunglasses and carrying his guitar. "What are you supposed to be?" Heather asked. "I don't remember any guitar players in *Alice in Wonderland*."

"I'm one of the Kingsmen." Zephyr strummed three chords on his guitar and sang a line from "Louie, Louie." He grinned. "Get it? The Kingsmen? Rock group most famous for 'Louie, Louie'?"

"I get it." Heather groaned.

"Leave it to Zephyr to come as a pun," Trish said.

"Better than wearing tights," he shot back.

"I want to see everyone out on the floor dancing," the DJ announced. "Remember, there's a prize for the best costume. This is your chance to show it off."

"Would you like to dance, Heather?"

Casey and Heather both turned to Hagan. "You're asking me to dance?" Heather asked.

"Yes. Would you like to dance?"

She put her hands on her hips. "After all those months when you wouldn't hardly look at me, now you ask me to dance? What's up with that?"

His lips curved in a hint of a smile. "Now that you're with Ben, I don't worry you'll take a simple dance the wrong way."

"So this is just a dance?" she asked.

He nodded. "If you don't say yes now, we'll have to wait until the next song."

"Yes." She gave him her hand and let him lead her onto the dance floor.

Casey chuckled and sat. "I hope Ben doesn't show up and see them dancing," she said. "He might get the wrong idea."

"Nah, not Ben," Trish said. "He's crazy about Heather. And he's known Hagan too long to believe he'd ever be serious about any local woman." She looked out over the dance floor. "Speaking of crazy, I don't see our Mad Hatter anywhere." She nudged Casey. "Where's Max?"

"How should I know?" Though Casey had been watching for him, too. Had he decided not to come in order to avoid running into her? But that was ridiculous. They saw each other all the time in town, though rarely in a social situation like this.

"Excuse me," Trish said. "He's your landlord. I thought he might have said something."

"No, he didn't say anything. Maybe he decided to skip the ball."

"Max hasn't missed a party—any party—in all the years he's been here. He wouldn't break his record now."

"That's a silly thing for a grown man to hold a record in," Casey snapped. One more reminder of why she and Max weren't right for each other. She could admit that truth, but she didn't have to be happy about it.

"Hey, lighten up," Trish said. "It's a party, remember?" She shoved a glass of punch toward Casey. "Don't worry about Max. He'll be here."

"I'm not worried about him." But, of course, she was.

Heather and Hagan returned from the dance floor, laughing. But when they reached the table, Heather immediately sobered. "No Ben?" she asked.

"Not yet," Trish said.

"Maybe he had an emergency with a patient," Casey said. "Did you try calling him?"

"I did," Heather said. "But the phone automatically goes to voice mail."

"Maybe he's in surgery," Hagan said.

"Maybe so." The words were a mumble.

Casey nudged her. "This is Ben we're talking about. He loves you. He's not standing you up."

"I know." Heather sighed. "It's silly, really. I just…I got the impression tonight was going to be really special." She glanced at Casey.

Casey's heart squeezed in sympathy for her friend. She

patted Heather's hand. "Don't worry about Ben. You can count on him, I'm sure." She stood. "I think I'm going to take a walk, get a little fresh air. You want to come with me?"

Heather shook her head. "No. I'll wait here." She stared toward the door. "He could still show up."

Casey slipped out the side door and into the clear night. She was glad Heather hadn't wanted to come with her. She needed some time alone to think things over. Tonight was kind of a turning point. She'd held on to the fantasy that at this ball, where costumes allowed everyone to reveal a little more of their true selves in the guise of playing a part, she and Max might find a middle ground—a way to work out their differences and focus on their love for each other. Obviously, that wasn't going to happen. She had to get used to the idea. No matter how much she tried to pretend otherwise, her life wasn't the same without Max in it.

MAX PARKED HIS JEEP crooked in a no-parking zone and shoved open the door. "You're going to get a ticket," Ben pointed out, not so helpfully.

"There's no other place to park." He leaned into the backseat and patted Molly. "You doing okay, girl?"

Molly opened one eye and looked at him drowsily.

"She'll be fine," Ben said. "She'll probably sleep the whole time we're inside."

Max climbed out and slammed the door. "If I get a ticket, I'll tell them I was driving a doctor on a medical emergency," he said.

"That's right," Ben said. "I always rush to my patient's sides dressed as a rabbit." He smoothed his whiskers with an exaggerated gesture.

Max settled his hat on his head. "At least you're in character. You're late."

"Very late." Ben checked the pocket watch that hung from a chain on his vest. "Heather's probably given up on me altogether."

"True love doesn't give up," Max said as they started across the parking lot.

"What would you know about it?" Ben said.

Max didn't answer, but found the back door into the Arts Center and opened it, holding it for his friend.

They spotted Hagan, Trish and the others seated at a table piled with empty glasses and bottles, paper plates and crumpled napkins. "Where have you two been?" Zephyr asked. For some reason, he was dressed like a waiter. Or maybe a big band leader.

"Doc had an emergency," Max said.

"Who was it?" Trish looked worried. "Anyone we know?"

"It was Molly." Ben sat next to Heather and patted her hand. "Sorry I was late."

"Molly? What is wrong with Molly?" Hagan asked.

"Hip dysplasia," Ben said. "Common in larger dogs. Nothing to worry about. I gave her some pain meds and anti-inflammatories that should hold her until Max can get her in to see the vet on Monday."

"You were late because you were taking care of Max's dog?" Heather asked.

Ben shrugged. "He begged me."

"Ben thinks she might need surgery on her hips," Max said. "I'm trying to talk him into performing the operation himself, but he refuses."

"I'm not a vet," Ben said, for maybe the twentieth time that night. "And don't you dare tell anyone else about tonight. I'll have half the people in the county showing up wanting free X-rays for their pets."

"How is Molly doing?" Trish asked.

"She seems okay. Still groggy." Max grinned. "We had to sedate her to take the X-rays. I don't know what she thought when she came out of it and there was a giant rabbit leaning over her. She'll probably have nightmares about it for months."

Ben stood and pulled Heather up beside him. "I'm not too late to dance with you, am I?"

"Never," she reassured him, and they headed for the dance floor.

"Where's Casey?" Max asked. He'd been searching for her since they entered the room, but hadn't been able to find her.

"She went for a walk." Trish looked around. "She's been gone awhile now. I hope she's okay." She glanced at him. "You didn't see her outside when you drove in?"

He shook his head. "Did she say where she was going?"

"No, just to get some air. She made it sound like she'd be back."

He shoved back his chair. "I think I'll just go make sure she's okay."

Out in the parking lot, he looked around, trying to decide where Casey might have gone. It was a long walk back to her place, but not an impossible one. Not very comfortable in heels, but doable.

But if she'd really only intended to get some air, he didn't think she'd head back to town. He turned instead toward the soccer fields alongside the Arts Center. He'd check in this direction first, then if he didn't find her, he'd head toward their apartments. He wouldn't be able to enjoy himself until he knew she was all right.

He hadn't gone far before a flash of red in the distance caught his eye. He quickened his pace and soon recognized Casey standing beside the dragon near the entrance to town, her long dress billowing in the breeze as she tilted her head up to regard the shining beast.

"Hey!" he called, running up to her. "I've been looking for you."

She turned to look at him. "Hi, Max. Why were you looking for me?"

"Everyone was worried. They said you'd been gone awhile."

She nodded. "I wanted to be alone for a little bit. To think."

Was she saying she wanted him to leave? Too bad. He was staying. "Molly wasn't feeling well this afternoon," he said. "The vet was closed, so I talked Ben into taking a look at her. That's why we were late."

"Is she okay?" Her voice rose in alarm. "What's wrong?"

"Ben says hip dysplasia. It's not life threatening, but she may need surgery. He gave her some drugs to make her feel better until she can see the vet on Monday. She's sleeping in the back of my Jeep right now."

"I hope she's going to be okay. She's such a sweet dog."

"She'll be fine. I'll take good care of her."

Her eyes met his for a moment, her look intense. "I know you will. You always do."

He couldn't look at her this way without wanting to kiss her and maybe say something that would come out all wrong. Instead, he turned to the dragon. "What are you doing way out here?" he asked.

"I drove by here the other day and for the first time I noticed something about this dragon. I wanted to see if I was right."

"What's that?" He studied the sculpture. He must have seen it hundreds of times. The red glass eyes glowed whenever they caught the light and the silver scales of the beast were positively blinding on a sunny day.

"The legs." Casey pointed toward the ground. "This huge beast is supported by these spindly little legs. It's ridiculous, really."

"Interesting." He studied the dragon's birdlike legs. What was she getting at here?

"There's a quote I've always liked, from this poet, Rainer Maria Rilke," she said. "It says 'Our fears are like dragons, guarding our deepest treasures.'" She glanced at him. "But if I think of my own fears like this dragon—without much to stand on—I realize how flimsy they are."

"What are you afraid of?" he asked.

She took a deep breath. "For a long time, I blamed all my problems on my parents, when the biggest problem was me," she said. "Instead of standing up for myself, it was easier to go along with everything they wanted, until I didn't know what I wanted anymore. That attitude almost ruined two lives—mine and Paul's."

"You can't say you're afraid anymore," he said. "You found the courage to stand up for yourself."

"So when are you going to find the courage to admit you're wrong?" she asked.

The words stunned him. He bristled. "Are you demanding an apology?"

She shook her head. "I'm not talking about me. I'm talking about *you*." She poked him in the chest. "You need to find the courage to admit you're wrong about yourself. You're as bad as I was, really, taking the easy way out instead of facing your fears."

He took a step back, not liking at all the direction this conversation was taking. "Are you saying I'm a coward?"

"I'm saying you're so afraid of disappointing others the way you think you've disappointed your parents that you've been hiding behind an image of the bad-boy black sheep. Let everyone think you're an irresponsible screwup and no one will ever expect anything of you. You won't ever have to risk failing at anything again."

Her words stung. He stared at her, unable to think of anything to say. Avoiding what you weren't good at wasn't cowardice—was it?

"The problem is," she continued, "the only one you're fooling is yourself."

"What are you talking about?"

She threw up her hands, exasperated. "You pretend you're not ambitious, yet how many men your age have their own successful businesses? You say you're not responsible, but you are. Everyone knows it but you won't admit it. Look how you've looked after Molly, staying home during mud season to deliver her puppies. You gave Zephyr a job because you knew he needed one. You volunteer with Search and Rescue, where you're responsible for other people's lives—people you don't even know. You take care of your friends." Her expression and the tone of her voice softened. "You've taken care of me. I wouldn't have settled into life here nearly as easily if you hadn't made it a point to introduce me to everyone and to make sure I was involved in everything."

She moved closer, her eyes locked to his. "You helped me realize that there was nothing wrong with living my own life," she said. "Even if it wasn't the life my parents had planned out for me. I wish I could make you see the same thing."

"You make me sound a lot better than I am," he said.

"No, I make you sound like exactly what you are." She moved closer still, her face turned up to his. "You don't have to be as educated as your brother and sister or as successful as your father. Those are their lives. You're successful at your own life. You're a good man, Max."

He wet his dry lips. "When you say it I believe it."

"Believe it." She stood on tiptoe and her lips touched his. He drew her into his arms and held her tightly, never wanting to let go. It was a long time before they drew apart. When they did, her eyes were shining.

"I've been doing a lot of thinking myself," he said.

"Oh?"

"Yeah." He took a deep breath, searching for the right words. He didn't want to screw this up. "I heard Paul came back to town," he said.

Her expression didn't change. "That's no secret."

He nodded. "I told myself it didn't matter—that I didn't have any claim on you. But the more people talked about it, the worse I felt." His hands tightened on her arms. "I had some really crazy thoughts. I wanted to find the guy and punch him—to tell him to keep his hands off of you because I was the one who loved you. Even though I'd done a lousy job of proving that to you."

"I know you love me, Max." She pressed her palm to his chest. "I never doubted it. The way I couldn't stop loving you."

Who would have believed those little words could make a man feel as if he were floating? He forced his thoughts back to the here and now, feet firmly planted on the ground. "I know I've been stupid," he said. "I had a lot of reasons for avoiding marriage, but I realize none of them were good ones. What did it matter if my parents didn't approve of my job or my friends—or my wife? They live a thousand miles away. Not to mention, they really liked you."

"I liked them, too." She smiled. "And I don't think they judge you as harshly as you judge yourself."

"Maybe so. I guess I had a lot of practice growing up. You fail enough times and you begin to believe you can't do anything right."

"You've done a lot right."

"I know. Maybe the best thing I ever did was falling in love with you." Before his nerve failed him, he sank to his knees and swept off his hat. He'd thought about this moment for a long time. He'd rappelled off cliffs, raced down steep bike trails and even steeper snow-covered mountainsides, but he'd never needed more courage than he did now. "I admit I've been a fool," he said. "It probably won't be the last time, but if you can live with that, would you marry me?"

Her smile transformed her face and her eyes shone with unshed tears. "Do you really mean that? You're sure?"

"Yes, I'm sure." He gave her a shaky smile. "I hear you've got a nice dress."

"Yes," she said. "Oh, yes." She tugged at his hands. "Now get up off the ground and kiss me."

He did as she asked, picking her up and whirling her around, her skirts a swirl of scarlet brushing against the dragon's scales. Together he and Casey would slay any dragons, real or imaginary, and find their own way to a happily ever after.

* * * * *

Look for more stories about Crested Butte, Colorado,
by Cindi Myers!
Watch for her next
Harlequin American Romance novel
in February 2008.

HARLEQUIN Romance.

New York Times bestselling author

DIANA PALMER

Handsome, eligible ranch owner Stuart York knew Ivy Conley was too young for him, so he closed his heart to her and sent her away—despite the fireworks between them. Now, years later, Ivy is determined not to be treated like a little girl anymore...but for some reason, Stuart is always fighting her battles for her. And safe in Stuart's arms makes Ivy feel like a woman...his woman.

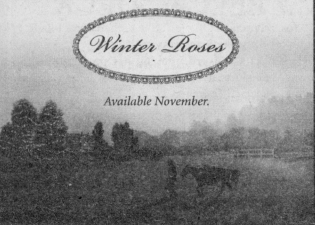

Winter Roses

Available November.

www.eHarlequin.com   HRIBC03985

HARLEQUIN®

Mediterranean NIGHTS™

Not everything is above board
on Alexandra's Dream!

Enjoy plenty of secrets, drama and sensuality
in the latest from Mediterranean Nights.

Coming in November 2007...

BELOW DECK

by

Dorien Kelly

Determined to protect her young son,
widow Mei Lin Wang keeps him hidden
aboard *Alexandra's Dream* under cover of
her job. But life gets extremely complicated
when the ship's security officer, Gideon Dayan,
is piqued by the mystery surrounding this
beautiful, haunted woman....

www.eHarlequin.com   HM38965

REQUEST YOUR FREE BOOKS!
2 FREE NOVELS PLUS 2
FREE GIFTS!

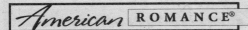 *American* **ROMANCE**®

Heart, Home & Happiness!

YES! Please send me 2 FREE Harlequin American Romance® novels and my 2 FREE gifts. After receiving them, if I don't wish to receive any more books, I can return the shipping statement marked "cancel." If I don't cancel, I will receive 4 brand-new novels every month and be billed just $4.24 per book in the U.S., or $4.99 per book in Canada, plus 25¢ shipping and handling per book and applicable taxes, if any*. That's a savings of close to 15% off the cover price! I understand that accepting the 2 free books and gifts places me under no obligation to buy anything. I can always return a shipment and cancel at any time. Even if I never buy another book from Harlequin, the two free books and gifts are mine to keep forever.

154 HDN EEZK   354 HDN EEZV

Name _____ (PLEASE PRINT) _____

Address _____ Apt. # _____

City _____ State/Prov. _____ Zip/Postal Code _____

Signature (if under 18, a parent or guardian must sign)

Mail to the **Harlequin Reader Service**®:
IN U.S.A.: P.O. Box 1867, Buffalo, NY 14240-1867
IN CANADA: P.O. Box 609, Fort Erie, Ontario L2A 5X3

Not valid to current Harlequin American Romance subscribers.

Want to try two free books from another line?
Call 1-800-873-8635 or visit www.morefreebooks.com.

* Terms and prices subject to change without notice. NY residents add applicable sales tax. Canadian residents will be charged applicable provincial taxes and GST. This offer is limited to one order per household. All orders subject to approval. Credit or debit balances in a customer's account(s) may be offset by any other outstanding balance owed by or to the customer. Please allow 4 to 6 weeks for delivery.

Your Privacy: Harlequin is committed to protecting your privacy. Our Privacy Policy is available online at www.eHarlequin.com or upon request from the Reader Service. From time to time we make our lists of customers available to reputable firms who may have a product or service of interest to you. If you would prefer we not share your name and address, please check here. ☐

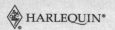

HARLEQUIN®

INTRIGUE®

Love can be blind...and deadly

On the night of her best friend's wedding, Laci Cavanaugh
saw that something just didn't seem right with Alyson's
new husband. When she heard the news of Alyson's
"accidental" death on her honeymoon, Laci was positive
that it was no accident at all....

Look for

THE MYSTERY MAN OF WHITEHORSE

BY B.J. DANIELS

Available November
wherever you buy books.

www.eHarlequin.com

HI69291

At forty, Maureen Hart suddenly finds herself juggling men. Man #1: her six-year-old grandson, left with her while his mother goes off to compete for a million dollars on reality TV. Maureen is delighted, but to Man #2— her fiancé—the little boy represents an intrusion on their time. Then Man #3, the boy's paternal grandfather, offers to take the child off her hands... and maybe even sweep Maureen off her feet....

Look for

I'm Your Man

by

SUSAN CROSBY

Available November wherever you buy books.

HARLEQUIN®

N**e**xt™

For a sneak peek, visit
TheNextNovel.com

HN88145

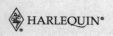

HARLEQUIN®

E V E R L A S T I N G   L O V E ™

Every great love has a story to tell™

Charlie fell in love with Rose Kaufman
before he even met her, through stories her
husband, Joe, used to tell. When Joe is killed
in the trenches, Charlie helps Rose through
her grief and they make a new life together.
But for Charlie, a question remains—can
love be as true the second time around?
Only one woman can answer that....

Look for

The Soldier and
the Rose

by
Linda Barrett

Available November wherever you buy books.

www.eHarlequin.com   HEL65421

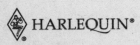

HARLEQUIN®

American ROMANCE®

COMING NEXT MONTH

#1185 THE PERFECT TREE by Roz Denny Fox, Ann DeFee and Tanya Michaels
There's something magical about sitting in front of a roaring fire, breathing in the rich sights and smells of a beautifully decorated Christmas tree. This holiday season, join three of your favorite Harlequin American Romance authors in three stories about finding love at a special time of year—and about finding the perfect Christmas tree.

#1186 DOWN HOME CAROLINA CHRISTMAS by Pamela Browning
Carrie Smith has seen her share of clunkers drive into her gas station in Yewville, South Carolina, but never has anything like movie star Luke Mason in his Ferrari shown up at the pump. And no matter how hard the sexy movie star tries to persuade her otherwise, she's positive Hollywood and Hicksville will never meet!

#1187 CHRISTMAS AT BLUE MOON RANCH by Lynnette Kent
Major Daniel Trent came to south Texas to be a rancher, although Willa Mercado doubts the injured veteran can handle the physical challenges of the life. She bets he'll back out of buying part of her ranch before their three-month agreement is up. But Daniel has every intention of spending Christmas—and the rest of his life—with Willa and her kids at Blue Moon.

#1188 ALL I WANT FOR CHRISTMAS by Ann Roth
Tina Morrell has her hands full when a dear family friend needs her help just as Tina's career in the cutthroat world of advertising takes off. But there's a surprise waiting for her back home on Halo Island—a single dad and a little girl who want to show her what the holiday season is really about....

www.eHarlequin.com

HARCNM1007